THE POWERS

HAVEN'S SECRET

BOOK ONE

MELISSA BENOIST & JESSICA BENOIST
WITH MARIKO TAMAKI

Cataloging-in-Publication Data has been applied for and may be obtained from the Library of Congress.

Hardcover ISBN 978-1-4197-5261-2
B&N Exclusive Edition ISBN 978-1-4197-6052-5

Jacket illustrations 2021 by Erwin Madrid
Text © 2021 Melissa Benoist and Jessica Benoist-Young
Book design by Deena Fleming

Printed and bound in U.S.A.
10 9 8 7 6 5 4 3 2 1

Amulet Books are available at special discounts when purchased in quantity for premiums and promotions as well as fundraising or educational use. Special editions can also be created to specification. For details, contact specialsales@abramsbooks.com or the address below.

Amulet Books® is a registered trademark of Harry N. Abrams, Inc.

ABRAMS The Art of Books
195 Broadway, New York, NY 10007
abramsbooks.com

For Grandma and Grandpa and our long drives through the mountains whistling to symphonies; you gave us our love of nature.

PROLOGUE

When it came for her, she didn't realize that she'd been slipping away piece by piece for a very long time. She only knew that the small things that once brought her joy—cold creek water rushing over her bare feet; the prick of a bramble on the pad of her finger; the soft, wrinkled nose of a newborn piglet; a human hand cupped in her own—those things no longer made her *feel*. That was how the Danger worked. It wriggled inside you and got to know your weakest parts. By the time you recognized its presence, there was nothing left to save.

Except.

The Danger had a blind spot. It did not know what it was like to love someone more than you loved yourself. It did not recognize the meaning of putting someone else first. And so for a while, she remained elusive. The Danger chipped away at her, but it had nowhere to burrow, take root, and flourish like the garden she carefully tended. That's how it went for a while: the girl running, the Danger chasing, the girl always one step ahead ... until the day she lost the thing she loved most in the world, and the Danger finally understood.

It met her in the woods behind the house. She knew it was coming. She knew better than to fight back. It made its presence felt in the swirling wind, the bending trees, the keening animals, the shadows cast by the waning moon. It filled her, and she let it. It fused to her body from the inside out, banishing all the parts she'd kept hidden and protected for so long.

She had thought she'd known what to expect, but the Danger filled her with an unimaginable emptiness—something far worse than the sadness of loss. It was the loss of self. She fought to wrest it back, realizing her mistake. She could have healed, grown stronger. The Danger had taken hold of her grief and tricked her.

It was too late, even for her.

Once, she had been trusted with unimaginable power.

Now, she was nothing.

And the Danger wasn't finished.

PART I:

A BROKEN PROMISE

CHAPTER ONE

On the morning of the day everything changed, Parker McFadden woke up at her usual time of seven o'clock, prepared to do all the things she normally did, because everything was still normal, for the most part. The first thing Parker saw when she opened her eyes was her room, which faced east. When she looked out her window and squinted, she could see the blue of the sky and the tips of the buildings between her house and the Pacific Ocean.

Parker's walls were painted a very satisfying, cheerful shade to mimic the cheerfulness of the outdoors. According to the swatch from the paint store, the color she'd chosen was Positive Vibes Yellow, and Parker had to agree. She wondered what it would be like to be the person who named paint for a living. She rolled onto her side and reached toward the shelf her dad had installed on the wall next to her bed for her necessities. Then she pulled out the thin notebook she kept stashed under an innocuous stack of novels. She turned to page fifty-six and searched for an empty spot, then jotted

"Paint Namer" in teeny-tiny print under "College Basketball Ref" and "Boatswain" in a list titled *Careers.* Then Parker tucked the notebook back in its spot, making sure to push it all the way in so you could barely see it beneath the larger books.

Parker could hear the slight rustling sound of her sister, Ellie, beginning to wake up in the bunk beneath her. According to the alarm on her phone, Parker had two more minutes before it was time to get up and face the world. She switched it off so it wouldn't ring, then lay back with a sigh. Parker always woke up two minutes before her alarm went off—it was her superpower. It was as if her subconscious brain wanted to eke out a couple of precious minutes of Parker being Parker and only that—not one half of Parker & Ellie. And today especially, she wanted to enjoy these first two minutes in peace.

Parker was buzzing with excitement. Energy coursed through her in a million tiny zaps. Any other day she might have jumped out of bed and hurried down to the kitchen. But today she stilled herself and took a deep breath, savoring the moment.

Today Parker was a newly minted twelve-year-old.

She stared at the wall next to her bed, then shifted her gaze to the wall at the bed's foot. Both spaces were covered in a collage of photos, pictures ripped from her parents' old magazines, posters, and art: an accumulation of the first eleven years of being Parker McFadden. But were they reflective of this new era? Would they hold up now that she was twelve? Probably not. Parker immediately began taking mental notes for a redesign.

On the wall adjacent Parker's bed, she had one WNBA poster from the 2008 season championships (for athletic inspiration); a picture of her and her sister at a park with their mom when they were small (her mom's face in profile, partially obscured by windswept hair); a photo of her ultimate frisbee team from last year when they won the championship (See! Inspiration works!); and one drawing of a red tulip—by her friend Clara—which Parker thought looked a little like a balloon, which was nice, because Parker preferred balloons to tulips. Beneath her, Parker heard a sleepy yawn. She glanced at her phone: one more minute left, all her own.

Then the door burst wide open, and Parker sat bolt upright in bed, nearly knocking her head on the ceiling. Ellie shrieked from the bottom bunk, where she'd been officially jolted out of sleep.

"Surprise!" shouted their dad, spilling into the room, his arms laden with gifts.

"DAD!" shouted Parker. "Don't you know anything about privacy?! WE ARE TWELVE NOW."

"Dad, I was sound asleep," mumbled Ellie so softly Parker could hardly hear her from up above.

"Sorry, sorry." At least he had the decency to look sheepish. Just then, Ellie's alarm started going off to the tune of birds chirping.

"Ahhhh!" shouted Parker.

"Ahhhh!" shouted Ellie. Parker peeked over the edge of the top bunk and saw her twin sister emerge from beneath a pile of blankets and fumble for her phone. She hit off, then glared at their father, insomuch as Ellie could glare. (She looked like an angry hedgehog, or something similarly adorable.) "Dad! I had one precious minute of sleep left!"

"Let me just try this again," their dad said, collecting the gifts from the floor and backing slowly out of the room. He tugged the door closed behind him. There was a long silence, followed by three short knocks. Ellie and Parker locked eyes. Ellie rolled hers, making Parker giggle. Parker snorted and stuck out her tongue, causing Ellie to collapse in a fit of laughter, her hair framing her face in an unruly crown.

Parker's heart thawed a little at that. Sometimes it wasn't so bad being half of Parker & Ellie. She brought a finger to her lips and Ellie's eyes widened, but she nodded. Then Parker slid out of bed and crept stealthily down the ladder to the ground below.

"Hello? Can I come in?"

"Just a second!" Ellie shouted, choking back laughter.

When Parker had both feet on the floor, she crept across the room toward the door. Then she nodded at Ellie.

"OK, Dad! You can come in now," Ellie called out.

Their dad opened the door slowly.

"Sur—"

"SURPRISE!" Parker shouted, leaping into his arms.

The packages went flying—again—and their dad caught her with an *oomph*. Then his foot snagged on the carpet and they both tumbled backward. A second later, Ellie jumped on top of them, knocking the wind out of Parker and making them all crack up. For a split second, everything felt perfect.

"Dad, you were super convincing this time," Ellie said. "For a second I thought you actually forgot we do this every single year."

"My acting skills are improving with old age." Their dad ruffled each of their hair. Then Parker spotted the gifts, lying abandoned on the bedroom floor, and her smile faltered at the reminder of their mom's absence. Part of her had thought this was the year everything would be different. That this year when their dad opened the door to surprise them, their mom would be right behind him, holding the gifts herself. But the only thing behind the gifts and her dad and Ellie—who was still rolling with laughter on the floor—was an empty hallway.

"Happy twelfth birthday, girls," their dad said, getting misty-eyed as he rose to his feet and offered a hand to each of them. "If only your mom could see you today! She would be so proud." If only *they* could see Mom today, Parker thought. She would have traded it for all the gifts in the world.

CHAPTER TWO

A minute later, Ellie, her sister, and their dad were settled atop Ellie's llama-print bedspread, which was the de facto gathering space in the girls' room, since it was on the bottom bunk. Their dad held two wrapped gifts in his lap, each only a little worse for wear from tumbling twice to the ground. The first was labeled, "To Ellie." The second, "To Parker."

"Well?" he asked expectantly from his perch at the end of Ellie's bunk. "Don't you want to see what Mom gifted you this year?"

Ellie smiled and nodded, but inside she was all twisted up. She did want to see. But also, she knew that whatever it was might make her sad. And she knew for sure it would make Parker mad. Every year when Dad delivered their special gift from Mom, Parker freaked.

"Why doesn't she hand it to us herself?" she always asked. "Takes a real coward to try to buy our forgiveness."

"Because she can't," Ellie always explained patiently, like it was a script she was reading from.

"Well, she's out there somewhere," Parker would say. "Obviously. How else would she have known to plan our birthday gifts in advance? It's because she left on purpose. And now she thinks a dumb gift every year will make up for it."

Ellie had spent a lot of time when she was a kid worried that terrible things would happen to Parker or their dad, because a terrible thing had happened to their mom. Their father had explained that their mother's circumstances were exceptional: She was an environmental activist who had a job working in places that were going through catastrophic events like fires and floods or the loss of entire animal populations. Still, one time when she was seven Ellie got so scared something would happen to their dad, she buried their father's car keys in their mom's old garden. It took ages to find them.

"She never would have left us if she could help it," Ellie told her sister year after year. The truth Parker couldn't accept was that their mom was dead. She'd left gifts because she had had a responsibility to help protect the planet when it was in peril. There had always been a chance she would not come back. And then one day, it had happened. Their dad had explained all that.

"Your mother was a brave person who died doing something she knew was dangerous but which she also knew was important," he told them. "But that doesn't mean something bad is going to happen to me."

If their mother was always running into dangerous situations, it made sense to Ellie that she had been prepared when it came to their birthdays. It meant she loved them *more*, not less.

After all, knowing when something bad was going to happen seemed to be something adults knew about.

And kids didn't.

Ellie was tired of having to explain it herself and tired of hearing Parker say, *Died scuba diving? Give me a break. That sounds like a story someone made up. Actually, it sounds like one of those stories she used to tell us when we were little. She probably made it up herself.*

"I'll take a pass on the present," Parker said now. "We're already late for school anyway. Clara said she was planning a surprise, and I want to get there before the first bell." She stared at the boxes like they might be holding tarantulas. (Which Ellie wouldn't have minded. Ellie thought all those furry legs moving this way and that had a delicate, graceful air. Were there ballerinas in the spider community? Probably.) Parker sounded irritated, but Ellie knew her sister's irritation wasn't about missing Clara's birthday surprise.

For their eighth birthdays, their mom had left them broken antique compasses. Parker had thrown hers in the trash, but Ellie had later retrieved it and kept it safe in her bureau.

For their ninth, an astrolabe, which was an ancient instrument that had to do with time and navigation and the positions of the stars, which even Parker had to admit was pretty cool.

For their tenth, two weather vanes, now installed in the backyard. Ellie's had a lion on top and Parker's had a circle with a cross inside. Their dad explained it was a symbol for earth. ("Why did you get the lion?" Parker had asked, looking envious.)

And for their eleventh, a whistle so high-pitched they couldn't hear the sound it made. ("This is pointless," Parker had said. "These are for dogs and we don't even have a dog." "I wish we had a dog," Ellie had responded, looking at their dad hopefully.) The gifts were treasured, if useless, artifacts from her mother's other life—the life that had taken her away from them. Ellie kept hers close, but she could understand why Parker didn't.

Still, it wasn't like Parker was the only McFadden twin who had secretly hoped their twelfth birthday would be different. When they were little, their mom had always made a huge deal about birthdays. She'd always talked about how twelve was a milestone in a kid's life—the cusp year—and how her own twelfth was her favorite birthday ever. When they asked why, she'd smiled mysteriously and said, "You'll see." Well, now they wouldn't see! It was hard not to be mad about it, even Ellie had to admit that. Turning twelve without their mom there was a weird feeling. Ellie felt all buzzy and excited to be twelve, but also sad their mom wasn't there to see it happen, and guilty for being buzzy at all. It was complicated.

"We've got plenty of time," their dad said.

Parker let out a dramatic sigh and shook the box her father handed her. Ellie accepted her own box gently, holding it in both hands like it might fall apart. She tried to guess its weight. The box itself was solid and heavy, but it fit easily in her cupped palms.

Parker began tearing off the wrapping paper, and Ellie followed suit. The gift wrap was clearly their dad's work, judging by how the ends weren't folded neatly like envelopes the way their mom used to do it. Instead, they were sort of crumpled up and affixed to the sides with several long pieces of tape.

Ellie tried not to picture the sapling that all that wasted paper represented. Parker discarded her wrapping in a pile for recycling, and Ellie folded hers neatly on the bed to reuse later. Then she stared. This present was very different from the other years' gifts.

She and Parker held two identical caramel-colored wooden boxes. A pattern of ornate swirls wound across the lids, forming a border. Inside each border were their initials, carved in fancy script. Each box was secured by a small brass buckle that needed to be twisted to release the catch.

Parker was already prying away the lid.

"One, two . . ." Ellie reminded her. Parker rolled her eyes, but paused; on "three," they opened their boxes simultaneously, like always. At first Ellie simply stared. She heard Parker's sharp intake of breath. Ellie glanced at her sister, who looked stunned.

Inside were delicate, gleaming silver bracelets. Parker's had one jagged edge, almost like a lightning bolt. Ellie's featured delicate swirls and a symbol that looked like rabbit ears. They were just like the one their mom had once worn except hers had been adorned with stars of various sizes. It had been the only trace of her remaining after her death.

The bracelets were lovely. And perfect. Somehow each bracelet captured the essence of Ellie & Parker.

"Wow," Parker whispered. She seemed at a loss for maybe the first time ever. "Did you know about these, Dad?"

He shook his head, smiling. "Your mom was full of secrets. But all her secrets were the good kind," he told them. "But here, don't forget her note."

Ellie slipped her bracelet around her wrist. It had looked a little big in the box, but once she had it on her wrist, it fit perfectly, almost as if it had adjusted to her size. It was loose, but somehow just snug enough that it wouldn't fall off. Parker whipped her arm around like a pinwheel, nearly hitting Ellie in the face while they searched through the castoff paper for a note.

Ellie found it first; it was tucked inside the lid of her box.

"Look!" she said to Parker. Her sister had one too.

The notes were scrawled on thick parchment and folded twice. The handwriting was clearly their mother's; there was no mistaking it. Ellie still had a whole stash from the Before days and from the gifts they'd received each year since.

> For my Ellie, on your twelfth birthday. Wear this bracelet always. Let it remind you to listen carefully. The magic will follow. Love, Mama.

Listen? Like listen to grown-ups? To their dad? Ellie was a little disappointed. She has never misbehaved. Maybe this note was really meant for Parker. She peered over Parker's shoulder. Her sister's mouth was set in a thin line. Parker shoved Ellie away, but not before she glimpsed the note.

"Hey!" Ellie said, rubbing her shoulder.

"Parker!" Their dad looked worried. "What was that about?"

"Nothing," Parker told him. "It's just my private note from Mom. I didn't want Ellie to see."

"Sorry," Ellie told Parker. Her stomach twisted for the second time that day. The twins used to share everything; there had been a time when there were no secrets.

"Me too," Parker mumbled.

"OK then," their dad said, rising to his feet. "Let's hurry! Birthday breakfast is in the works." He padded out the door and down the stairs, his slippers shuffling in their familiar, comforting way.

"Race you," Parker told Ellie, like she always did. And as she always did, Ellie ignored her and walked across the room to feed her goldfish, Walter, instead. She heard the bathroom door slam shut. Ellie reached for the fish flakes and dropped some into Walter's bowl. She squinted through the glass for Walter; the water was especially murky. Then she realized: She had not changed his water the night before, which meant she'd have to do it when it was her turn in the bathroom, which would make them even later for Parker's birthday surprise.

Ellie did not want to mess up Parker's morning. But one thing about having a fish was worrying about doing something that might accidentally hurt him, like not changing his bowl water, or changing the water and making it too hot or too cold. Walter's health was more important, Ellie reasoned, especially since Parker's surprise could probably happen just as easily after first period. Ellie would just have to be quick.

While she watched Walter gobble his flakes and waited for Parker to finish her shower, she employed a technique her mother had taught her to use when she was little when she was nervous.

She began talking to herself.

Technically speaking, she was talking to Walter (because he was there) *and* to herself.

"Walter," Ellie whispered as her fish swam laps around his plastic castle. "It's my twelfth birthday. I thought today would be special, but so far everything is mostly the same." Walter stopped circling the castle and moved to the front of the bowl, looking at her as if he sympathized. Walter was a goldfish with one white fin, one yellow fin, and extremely intelligent eyes. He really looked as if he understood Ellie.

"Did you know," Ellie said, changing topics to one that was less gloomy, "that underneath the forest floor is a network of mushrooms? And the mushrooms are like telephone lines that let the trees talk to each other? I think that's quite something. It makes you think of how many things are actually alive and talking to each other."

In past water bowl chats, Walter would just swim in his bowl or glass and make his normal mo-mo-mo face—a face Ellie found comforting—but on that morning, he didn't just make his mo-mo-mo face. His little mouth opened and closed, then opened and paused. He held it there for a long time, longer than was typical. For a second, Ellie remembered her mom's words: *listen carefully ... the magic will follow.* Her heart accelerated.

"What is it, Walter?" she asked the fish. But he merely closed his mouth and let out a little gurgle of air just as Parker spun back through the room like a tempest bundled in a bathrobe. Ellie blinked. Walter probably just didn't want to drink the gross water.

"Your turn," Parker told her, already rummaging through her bureau.

Ellie glanced around their room, which was perfectly bisected: on one side, Positive Vibes Yellow and covered in picture collages; on the other side, Mousy Mossy Green with a few shelves for succulents and books and a desk for framed photos, school supplies, and Walter's bowl. Nothing about the two sides was alike, other than the fact that they were part of the same space.

As Ellie carefully lifted Walter's bowl, slipped out the door, and padded down the hallway to the bathroom, she admired the beautiful bracelet on her wrist and thought about Parker's own wrist, which Ellie had glimpsed while Parker was towel-drying her hair. Parker had wanted to hide her note from Ellie, but Ellie had been too quick. She knew what it had said. Which made the sight of Parker's wrist—completely bare—hurt all the more.

CHAPTER THREE

Parker couldn't believe how mad she was. It wasn't even eight o'clock, and she was furious as a tempest. Her mom's note had simply read, *Wear this bracelet always. Let it remind you that your sisterhood comes first. The magic will follow.* But what did her mom know about it? She'd been an only child and she hadn't even been around for the last five years of Parker being Parker & Ellie. Some sisterhood.

When Ellie and Parker were five, Parker had fallen off the swing set at the playground down the street and sprained her wrist. It was just two years before their mom supposedly went on a scuba diving mission to study the endangered fin whale population off the coast of California and never returned. (Death by scuba diving! It was too random to sound believable, but also impossible to disprove.) When she cried, Ellie lost it, and Parker had to stop crying in order to help Ellie calm down. Still, Ellie was inconsolable the entire way to the hospital, and she still was even in the room with Parker and their mom and the doctor. When their dad met them there and ushered Ellie out the door to get the girls ice cream from the hospital café, Parker was glad to finally be alone with their mom. The doctor was nearly finished with Parker's splint when Parker spat out, "Why does Ellie have to be such a baby? She's not even the one who's hurt."

Parker's mom had looked at her carefully, and was silent for a while. It was probably only a minute, but it was long enough for Parker to feel a hot flush work its way from her neck to her cheeks. She knew what she had said was mean. "Parker," her mom said—and Parker could see the disappointment in her eyes—"your sister feels things deeply, because that's how much she loves you. Your pain is her pain. You may think you're the stronger one, but your sister's compassion makes her strong too. You need her just as much as she needs you." Then Parker heard Ellie and their dad return with the ice cream, and Ellie proudly brandished a bowl of half moose tracks, half rainbow sherbet (a mix of her and Parker's favorites). Parker's mom greeted them with a big smile—one that matched Ellie's—and Parker's heart suddenly hurt more than her wrist.

Parker had been rummaging fruitlessly through her bureau for something to wear. Now she gave up on that and reached into her closet instead, shuffling amongst piles of dirty clothes until she located her ultimate frisbee uniform, which she slipped on in all of sixty seconds using a method she'd timed. Once she was dressed, she pulled her long, dark hair into a ponytail and pulled on her favorite rainbow high-tops, which she kept by the door. She grabbed the wooden box from where she'd left it beneath Ellie's bed and dropped the silver bangle, which she'd discarded atop her bureau, back inside. *Wear this bracelet always.* Well, their mom wasn't there anymore, was she? No. She'd disappeared without so much as a goodbye. So Parker could wear the bracelet when she felt like it. She put the box in the bureau beneath a stack of days-of-the-week underwear and a hidden stash of *Star Wars*–themed Pez dispensers and felt only the tiniest bit guilty when she headed downstairs, her wrist bare.

When she entered the kitchen, Parker's dad was on the phone (as usual) talking with someone from work. Mr. McFadden was so tall he practically had to fold himself in half to fit in the breakfast nook. He was all limbs under the table, and above it, his phone was pressed to his ear and his thick hair came just an inch from grazing the nook's slanted ceiling. Parker had inherited his height, which was awesome, because it gave her an advantage in many sports. Her reach was excellent for serving in tennis, and she could hit a perfect volleyball spike like no one else at Harborville Middle School. Parker was grateful for this, but when she sometimes caught a glimpse of her mom in Ellie's fine-boned features, it made her feel diminished.

Dad looked stressed out. Parker wondered if it was from the call he was on or from the morning's commotion with the gifts. Whatever the cause, his glasses were smudged, and his black hair stuck up in chaotic tufts as he tapped his fingers on the table the way he always did when Something Was Up.

"Are you sure?" His brow furrowed, and he lowered his voice. "I know. I know it has to happen eventually. I just don't know that now is—"

Parker took another step into the kitchen and her dad looked up, spotting her, and cleared his throat. Then he forced a smile and held up one finger. *Just a minute,* he mouthed in her direction. Parker noticed his coffee was half drunk in his mug and—sure enough, when she picked it up—the mug was cold. She popped it back in the microwave and set the timer for one minute.

"We'll go over the details this afternoon," he said, before hanging up abruptly. The microwave dinged, and Parker retrieved his coffee, placing it on a napkin so her dad wouldn't ring the table with coffee spills.

"Thanks, Sweet P," he said distractedly, taking a long sip.

Parker's memories of her mother could be numbered in the single digits, but she knew Ginny Power considered breakfast the most important meal of the day. And she'd especially liked breakfast on holidays and birthdays, because it was an excuse for whipped cream. In fact, she was the one who had started the pancake breakfast birthday tradition. Speaking of which . . . Parker glanced around the kitchen. There was a bag of chocolate chips on the counter next to a big mixing bowl, but no stack of warm pancakes awaited her at the table the way they always did on the twins' birthday.

"Dad, where are our birthday pancakes?"

"Oh shoot." He looked stricken. "That call completely derailed me. And now we have"—he glanced at his watch—"only fifteen minutes before we have to leave for school. How about we have pancakes for dinner tonight instead? We can go to Maggie's, and you and your sister can have sundaes for dessert. I packed you cupcakes for lunch," he added hopefully. "With a side of baby carrots."

Dad had never been the best meal planner, but cupcakes for lunch? Diner pancakes for dinner? Sundaes for dessert? Even for a birthday, that was weird. Something *was* up, for sure. In the old days, Parker would have made a mental note to discuss this with Ellie later.

"I thought you had to work tonight," Parker pointed out. "Remember? We were going to do birthday dinner tomorrow. And I was going to grab burgers with Clara after Ultimate practice today. She even invited Ellie to come." *Since Ellie doesn't have friends of her own,* she didn't add.

Her dad ran his hand through his hair. "Something came up for tomorrow, so I called out of work tonight," he explained. "I hope that doesn't ruin your plans with Clara." Now her dad looked so upset with himself that Parker gave him the biggest grin she could muster and reached for the box of granola in the pantry, feigning enthusiasm.

"No problem. Maggie's it is. And I was kind of craving granola for breakfast anyway." Hopefully, Ellie wouldn't freak. Ellie was all about honoring their mom's traditions, because Ellie still believed their dad's cover story about their mom dying tragically near Bodega Bay rather than abandoning them heartlessly for a new life and trying to buy their forgiveness with weird, obscure birthday gifts.

Parker was a realist. Ellie had her head in the clouds. Ellie and Parker were about as related as people could get without being identical. But if you looked at them it wasn't super obvious. Maybe they were twins, but exactly zero parts of them were identical—from Ellie's ideals and the wide green eyes she'd gotten from their mom, to Parker's stubbornness and the long, gangly limbs she'd inherited from their dad. Aside from the same shade of brown hair, they looked nothing alike.

They were similar in certain small ways. They liked the same food—particularly anything with fake cheese, anything spicy, anything with real cheese, and anything with matcha. They both liked extra lemon in their fizzy water and extra, extra fudge sauce on their sundaes. They had the same sneeze, and the same laugh that used to echo down the upstairs hallway when they were younger and stayed up all night talking and being silly.

When it came down to it, though, Ellie was all Power and Parker was all McFadden, and Parker figured that was why Ellie was so determined to think the best of Ginny Power. Well, Parker was strong enough to handle the truth.

And the truth right now was that, so far, being twelve wasn't magical at all. That was just another one of their mom's lies. Twelve sucked. Parker poured some granola into a bowl and added milk from the fridge. Personally, she thought granola was a weird excuse for eating nuts and raisins in milk or yogurt. But her mom had liked granola and therefore Ellie liked granola, so it was always just sort of . . . around.

Parker slipped into the nook next to her dad and watched the news while she ate. Dad always left the TV on through breakfast because he liked to see the weather report, or the fluffy cloud and yellow dot on the screen that told him it was going to be a balmy day in Harborville, California.

While she munched on her blah cereal, Parker messaged with her best friend, Clara, her de facto sister.

Parker: Hellloooooooo

Clara: 🦔 🍠

Parker: 😃

Clara: ❤️ 🎉

"Hm," Parker's dad muttered from next to her, breaking her concentration. "Seems like storms are brewing up north." It was true. Gray thunderclouds saturated the part of the map that indicated Washington, Oregon, and the west coast of Canada. "Unusual," her dad said, looking concerned. "Those are some fierce winds."

"Really?" Parker straightened. "Do you think it'll come down here?"

Her dad looked at her as if he'd forgotten she were there.

"No!" he exclaimed, relaxing his brow. "Of course not. We almost never get big storms in Harborville, you know that."

By the time Ellie finally joined them downstairs, Parker was finished with her granola and she and Clara had sent each other all the good emojis, including the hedgehog and Parker's personal favorite, the bisected yam. But Ellie being late was nothing new. If Parker felt time the same way she felt the ground beneath her feet, Ellie seemed to feel time the way a person sees air. Which was to say . . . Ellie did not seem to think much of time at all.

Ellie's arrival in the kitchen was preceded by a series of mysterious thumps and bumps that rattled the ceiling above the eating nook. It sounded as if she were playing volleyball in her bedroom with three balls and concrete high tops. Except that Ellie hated sports.

Thump. Thump! Thump thump thump.

And Parker *loved* sports. Especially Ultimate.

Mere minutes before they had to leave, like an unexpected hurricane not reported by Darla Davenport on KQED News, Ellie slid into the kitchen looking like she'd never seen it before. As usual, Ellie looked like she'd put her clothes on while blindfolded. Her bangs were going every which way, some sticking up in tufts. Her T-shirt was wrinkled, which made sense, since it was the same one she'd slept in. One earring was missing, and her book bag sagged open where she'd forgotten to zip it.

Oh, and she had *one* shoe tucked under her arm. The other was on her foot, but untied.

And somehow the shoe she did have on—the untied one—was making *squitching* sounds with each step she took on the yellow kitchen tile.

"Pancakes?" Ellie asked hopefully.

"We're doing them tonight," Parker explained.

"Oh." Ellie looked disappointed. Then she brightened. "I think we have granola!" She ran to the cupboard enthusiastically while their dad fished around for a clean bowl and, coming up empty, washed one in the sink for Ellie to use.

"I'll pick you up at school after Parker's Ultimate scrimmage, then we can go to Maggie's for pancake dinner," he said. "I have to work, so I can't go to the scrimmage."

Of course he did. Ever since their mom went away, he worked all day and all night, even on weekends, except for birthdays and certain holidays.

"Ellie, you'll support your sister, right?"

"Um." Ellie blinked. "Sure." She shot Parker a small smile.

The truth was, Parker's Ultimate scrimmage was probably the last place Ellie wanted to be after school on her birthday.

Sometimes, when Parker caught herself getting frustrated with Ellie, she would try and think of those things they shared. Like their new, matching silver bracelets, which Ellie was now nervously twirling as she stared pointedly at Parker's bare wrist.

"We have about two minutes." Parker gave her sister a look. "Breakfast?"

"Yeah! I'll be quick." Ellie heaved her bag up on the counter.

But as soon as Ellie turned toward the fridge for some milk, her bag fell, and a stream of nuts spilled out of the open front pocket and onto the floor.

"Nuts!" Ellie exclaimed.

Ellie dropped to the floor to scoop up the spray of almonds now scattered there. Parker pulled out her phone to text Clara.

PARKER: My sister is a PISTACHIO.

CLARA: Your sister is a BAG OF PISTACHIOS.

PARKER: My sister's bag is LITERALLY full of nuts she just spilled on the floor.

Parker's father turned to them and blinked, seeming suddenly aware of the chaos around him. He shook his head. "What happened here? Oh, never mind. We'd better get this cleaned up pronto, or we're going to be late."

It took five minutes for all three of them to get everything back in Ellie's bag, which was full of crumpled bits of paper and leaves. Parker was getting anxious. She was never going to get to her locker in time to see Clara's surprise.

Shoving fistfuls of nuts into her bag, Ellie looked up at Parker.

"Sorry," she whispered, in the tone Parker recognized as please-don't-be-mad-at-me.

"It's OK," Parker said. It was wild how Ellie could read her mind. She pulled Ellie to her feet and managed a smile. "We just need to hurry."

Ellie spent the ride staring out the window while Parker snuck in a few extra texts before school. Another thing they agreed on was that their father's taste of morning driving music—the Doobie Brothers and Led Zeppelin—was terrible.

Clara: Get ready for your BIG DAY!

Parker: I was BORN ready.

Clara: You were BORN today. 😄 😄

Parker: 🥚 🦄 ⚡

Clara: Hey is your dad playing 😫 tunes?

Parker: Guess.

The car skidded to a stop in front of school with a minute to spare before the first bell. Parker leapt out of the car, jogging in place while Ellie gathered her stuff.

"OK?" she asked, looking at Ellie. "Coming?"

"Go ahead without me," Ellie replied. Then she blinked like the thought had just been dropped into her head like a penny. "Hey. Um. Good luck at the scrimmage."

"Thanks!"

And with that, Parker bolted toward the school, darting into the crowd of students. She spotted Clara from a distance and broke into a gallop, grinning as she slammed into her unsuspecting best friend.

"GAAHHH!" Clara hollered, punching Parker in the arm. "Happy birthday, Tornado Face! Hurry up and open your locker!"

Parker fumbled with her lock, eager to see what Clara had done. Last year, she'd filled the whole thing with mini disco balls and lollipops. Parker's palms were sweaty with anticipation and also nerves, because she hated being late for class, and the groups of students crowding the hall were already beginning to trickle away. Finally the latch clicked, and her locker door swung open.

"Ahhhh!" Parker shrieked, covering her face. But it was the best kind of shriek, because Clara had printed out dozens of actual, nondigital photos of the two of them and covered Parker's locker door with them. There was the first time they'd been tall enough to ride a roller coaster, Clara's dark curls practically filling the frame. There was the time Parker had joined Clara and her moms for a camping trip at Yosemite, and Parker had let a worm crawl up her arm and hang out there for a while instead of using it as bait. There they were taking a selfie at the movies, Clara's cheeks so full of popcorn they'd coined the nickname "Girlbil."

Parker might have cried if a cascade of Butterfinger minis—her favorite—hadn't poured out, and if two glittery balloons weren't fighting to escape. Parker tugged at their strings to free them: a giant 1 and a giant 2. She looped the ribbons through the outside handle of her locker and threw her arms around her best friend.

"You are awesome."

"That's not all the surprises!" Clara exclaimed. "Miss Connell posted *the list*."

Parker's jaw dropped. "She wasn't supposed to post it until next week!" Parker scooped up her books and shoved the candy back into her locker, closing the door tight just as the first bell rang. Clara wiggled her eyebrows and grabbed Parker's hand, pulling her in the direction of homeroom.

Parker's heart thudded as they approached the door. Sure enough, there was a piece of paper tacked to the bulletin board outside the classroom. A cluster of kids huddled around it.

"Parker!" Nonie, a blond girl several inches shorter than Parker, flipped her braids over her shoulder. "You made it to CUT!" The other girls burst into cheers.

"I made it too," Clara told her, offering parker a high five.

"No," Parker said with a gasp. "No. Freaking. Way."

"Yes way," Clara told her. "See for yourself! We're going to spend all summer kicking the crap out of Competitive Ultimate Training camp."

Nonie and the others stepped aside so Parker could approach the list. There it was: Parker McFadden, three spots above Clara Rutledge.

"Holy crap." Parker was stunned. It was what she'd worked for all season. And now it was here. Real. She blinked back tears. She *never* thought she'd make the cut for CUT. She hadn't even told Ellie about it because she didn't want to jinx it. Twelve didn't suck after all! This was officially the best, most perfect birthday ever.

Her mind flashed back to the silver bangle, stuffed in her drawer at home. And to Ellie, who probably had her nose in a book in her homeroom at the opposite end of the school. "Ha!" she shouted, pumping her fist in the air. "*This* is how the magic happens!"

"Come on, Hot Pants." Clara grinned and grabbed Parker's sleeve, hauling her into class. "We're late for homeroom."

CHAPTER FOUR

Even though they were in the same grade, Ellie and Parker had very different experiences of school. Harborville was a bustling metropolis on the southern California coast. There were 2,056 kids in their class and 10,000 total in the whole middle school. And theirs wasn't the only middle school in Harborville, or even the only *public* middle school in Harborville.

Being what it was, the campus was huge, and the girls' homerooms were in opposite ends of one of the buildings. They had different lunch hours and schedules, something their principal had convinced their dad was necessary for "individual growth." They almost never saw each other, except for occasionally passing each other in the hallway between classes. People were always surprised to find out they were twins when it came up, which it hardly ever did.

The *real* twins in school (or at least, the ones everyone talked about) were Casey and Cassie Phillips. They were in ninth grade in the upper school. They were extremely popular, and even the seventh-grade teachers reminisced about having "the Twins" in class, as if they were a collective unit (and the only such unit around). "The Twins," who were Japanese American with traces of an Irish accent they'd inherited from their dad, looked a lot alike with their dark hair, even features, farmer-chic wardrobes, and matching brown eyes. They did everything together except for sports, which were still not coed. But they chose the same types of sports so they could practice together. They were both members of the swim team, lacrosse team, debate club, student council, Asian American Alliance, dance squad, and SFABE (Students for a Better Earth). For some reason individual growth wasn't a priority for *their* curriculum.

Without Parker to make Ellie feel a part of something, school to Ellie was like being an animal in a not-well-maintained zoo. Everyone was always moving and yelling, and it seemed like everyone knew something Ellie didn't know about how to be a kid—like what drink you were supposed to have with lunch, where the appropriate rips were in jeans, and when it was or wasn't OK to add ketchup. A few months ago, everyone did something to their hair that Ellie still couldn't figure out and was too embarrassed to ask anyone to explain.

When Ellie was younger, her mom had handled these types of murky scenarios. For example, in the first grade, everyone who didn't have pierced ears suddenly wore stick-on earrings. Ellie never would have noticed something like that, but her mom had taken one look around Ellie's classroom at drop-off, and the next morning both Ellie and Parker had stick-on glitter hearts on their nightstands when they woke up.

Ellie's dad did his best, but he didn't have their mom's keen sense of what kids were supposed to do at any given age. He said kind, unhelpful things like, "Be yourself, L-Bean, and everything will fall into place." Parker just sort of *knew,* like their mom had, but she tended not to notice that Ellie didn't know.

The only thing Ellie truly enjoyed about school was science class with Mrs. Chang in sixth period at the very end of the day. Mrs. Chang's lab smelled like formaldehyde and dirt—a combination of odors that was both overpowering and oddly appealing to Ellie.

Mrs. Chang was not much taller than Ellie, and she wore sweaters with holes in the sleeves and Birkenstocks. When she wasn't talking, she was leaning on her desk at the front of the classroom and reading. Her glasses were always smudged. Ellie often pictured Mr. Chang as the same person as Mrs. Chang, only with less hair. Like a set of nerdy salt and pepper shakers who ate dinner while reading. Ellie hoped one day she would find her pepper to read and eat with.

Mrs. Chang let Ellie do special projects and gave her books on mushrooms and explained how mushrooms are an underground information highway. She even let Ellie grow fungus samples in the back of the class. Ellie's classmates wrinkled their noses and called it Ellie Mold. But watching it get bigger and fuzzier every day was relaxing. If you looked closely, you could see all the threads of mushroom reaching out, connecting with other threads. Talking.

Mrs. Chang told Ellie that people would appreciate her more when she was older, but that on the whole, people were overrated. Ellie didn't know what she thought about that.

"This planet would be a better place if it were mostly plants," Mrs. Chang said. "Plants understand that they are part of the ecosystem, part of the give and take of the world. It's a basic concept that humans tend to forget. At least, the 'give' part."

Ellie thought about this. "What about animals?" she asked.

Mrs. Chang shrugged. "I'm allergic to cats," she said.

Ellie was equally pro plant and animal, and she wanted to give humans the benefit of the doubt, but she did not discuss this with Mrs. Chang. Mrs. Chang seemed to think Ellie was weird in a smart way, and Ellie *was* smart enough to know the difference between socially awkward and something Mrs. Chang might have to call Ellie's dad about.

After science class ended, Ellie wanted to go to Parker's scrimmage, but she also worried that she wouldn't know where to sit or when to cheer, and she didn't want to embarrass Parker. So instead, she sat on the steps at the front of the school and fed the squirrels while she waited for their dad to pick them up. Squirrels were as fascinating as fungus to Ellie, because of their little hands and their quivering noses and their tails. Like Mrs. Chang, squirrels generally did not like people, but they like nuts—and they seemed to like Ellie if she sat still while holding nuts. Ellie knew if she was patient and gentle, they would eventually trust her and take the nut right from her hand.

"It's OK," she whispered, holding out her hand. "I won't hurt you."

Every once in a while, Ellie could hear cheers and shouts coming from the direction of the athletic fields. Sometimes, if she thought about Parker, she could feel Parker's hum in the distance. The hum was magnified when Parker was playing sports. It wasn't that Ellie wasn't good at sports; in fact, she was an excellent swimmer. But there was a difference between swimming in a lake or ocean surrounded by hundreds of organisms and swimming in a cold, chlorine-sterilized pool with a bunch of kids who wanted to "win."

All these thoughts were running through Ellie's head when Parker appeared in front of her, her cheeks flushed from running around. Clara was standing next to her, hands on her hips.

"Hi, Ellie." Clara waved.

"Hi." Ellie sat on her hands, trying to conceal the remainder of her nuts.

"Dad says he'll be here in two minutes. Did you see his text?" Parker sounded impatient, but not in a bad way. More like she was eager to stay in motion.

Their dad pulled up before Ellie had a chance to reply. Parker and Clara dashed over to the car, and Ellie left her handful of nuts for the squirrels to finish, then gathered her things.

"I think it ought to just be us three this evening," Ellie's dad was explaining when Ellie approached.

"But why?" Parker looked confused.

"It's OK, Mr. McFadden," Clara said, before he could answer. "My mom is on her way anyway. Parker, we'll do a special birthday thing this weekend!"

Ellie thought she saw her dad wince a little as Clara wrapped Parker in a hug.

"Say hi to your moms for me," he called after Clara when she and Parker parted.

"Will do." Clara smiled and offered them a wave before heading back over to the school steps.

"Are you OK?" Ellie asked her dad, as she slid into the front seat. He nodded and gave her hand a pat.

"Just fine, L-Bean." But his fingertips were *tap-tap-tapp*ing on his leg, and he didn't look just fine at all. Ellie felt *something* that she couldn't put her finger on. She remembered her mom's note: *listen.* But what if the thing she was supposed to be listening for was something she didn't want to hear?

CHAPTER FIVE

Maggie's House of Breakfast was one of the only places in Harborville that served breakfast twenty-four hours per day. You could also get nonbreakfast items like Salisbury steak (not that anyone wanted to) or mozzarella sticks, but Parker always stuck to a cheese omelet with a side of pancakes and whipped cream. Maggie's was reserved for particular occasions: weekends, a lift-up after tough things (like when Parker broke her ankle during field hockey and had to have it set), and report card dinners (assuming both Parker and Ellie had worked hard and tried their best). They had never gone on Parker and Ellie's birthday, though. But the unspoken rule they had about Maggie's was, above all, they only went there for happy occasions. It was a huge surprise, then, when out of nowhere Parker's dad started talking about Great-aunt Mabel and Great-uncle George like it was no big deal.

Of the millions of things a person could talk about at Parker's favorite breakfast place, this particular subject would have been last on her guess list.

Her dad didn't even bring it up during the hour (standard) that they were waiting outside with the hipsters for a table. (Maggie's didn't accept reservations, even for birthdays.) Or while they were opening the rest of their gifts as their food was being prepared. He waited until Parker was about to dig into her favorite pancakes, one of Maggie's specialties, the Anything You Want Pancakes, that Parker had loaded up with blueberry, ginger, and chocolate chips (Ellie's were peanut, banana, and chocolate chips).

"I have some news," he said, sipping his coffee. "Actually a few pieces of news. The first is, we're about to get a visit from Great-aunt Mabel and Great-uncle George."

Ellie paused, her spoon hovering above her bowl of rice pudding. She squished her eyebrows together. "When?"

Her father sipped his Diet Coke. "Tomorrow."

Parker almost choked on her pancake. "Tomorrow?! Who are these people? Have we even met them?"

"You met them once, when you were babies," their dad said, avoiding her eyes. "They're your mom's aunt and uncle— they're brother and sister."

Parker looked over at Ellie, who sipped her orange juice and didn't seem too perturbed. Parker turned to stare at her father. "Our aunt—?"

"Great-aunt . . ." Ellie clarified.

"Great-aunt Mabel and Great-uncle George"—Parker

took a sip from her water glass—"whom we've basically never met before . . . will be here tomorrow?"

"Yes." Her father placed his hands on the table.

"What for? Are they in town on a trip?" Ellie asked.

"Well. Actually, that's the other part of the news . . ." Her father paused to rub his face, which was something Parker had seen him do on really difficult phone calls. He sighed. "Girls, Mabel and George aren't just coming for a visit. They are coming to spend time with you. You know how I'm always being asked to cover international events for the *Tribune*? But I always turn them down because you need me at home?"

"Yes," said Ellie. She looked solemn. Parker didn't say anything. Of course he turned these things down. Who was supposed to take care of them? Ellie's goldfish?

"Well," he went on. "I have decided to accept a long-term assignment in Holland."

"WHAT!" Parker screeched, dropping her fork into her mush of pancakes. She had a million questions to ask, but her throat was too tight. Why hadn't he asked them what they thought? How long would he be gone? Why had he made a huge decision without seeing how she and Ellie felt?

"How long-term?" Ellie asked calmly. But Parker could see she was worried.

"Eight weeks," their dad said. "Just the summer. And I'm going to try to come back once in the middle, if I can. I know it seems abrupt, but the truth is, the offer came in several months ago, in January. I turned it down because I can never stand being away from you girls." He took a deep breath. "But then they came back to me and doubled their offer. This will give us a lot of financial security. Enough so I can spend more time with you in the future. I can cheer you on at Ultimate, Parker. And I can help you plant a garden out back, Ellie. You'll see, it'll be good for us in the long run."

"I don't want you to go," Ellie said in a small voice.

"Oh, L-Bean." Their dad grabbed each of their hands. "I don't want to go either, if I'm being honest. I'd much rather spend my summer at home with you. But the truth is, your mother wanted this for you."

Parker and Ellie exchanged a look.

"Mom wanted you to abandon us and move to Europe? What does this have to do with Mabel and George?" Parker demanded, retrieving her hand.

"Mom wanted you to spend some time with her side of the family," he explained. "It was very important to her that you get to know Mabel and George when you were old enough. She spent a lot of time with them when she was a kid, and she was crazy about them."

"Then how come we've never met them?" Parker asked. "If Mom loved them so much."

"Because they lived all over the country. They've always been far-flung."

There were too many things going on at once. Mabel and George were visiting . . . she had to get to know them for some reason . . . her dad was going away . . . Parker felt the same kind of overwhelming sensation she felt when Mr. Gifford sprang a pop quiz in math. Like nothing made any sense, and things were way too daunting, and she only wanted to lay her head on her desk and fall asleep and figure it out later. Then she remembered something.

"Well, I won't be around anyway," Parker informed them. "Sorry, Ellie. You're on your own." Parker knew she was being a little mean. But she wasn't going to give up Competitive Ultimate Training for anything. She had been meaning to share her good news over sundaes, until her announcement got hijacked by this *other* news.

"Oh shoot." Her dad ran his hand through his hair. "I completely forgot you tried out for CUT. I'm so sorry, Parker. You'll have to wait till next year."

"But *why?*" Parker's voice was so loud the couple at the table next to them looked over. She could feel her face getting hot, the way it always did when she was upset. In fact, her whole body was hot. Her summer was going to be perfect. It was all planned. Her dad couldn't do this to her.

"This was what your mom wanted," her dad repeated. "And it's time."

"Why is it time?" Ellie wanted to know. "We just turned twelve this morning. Is this what happens when you become a grown-up? Things just . . . happen, even if you don't want them to?"

Their dad laughed. Parker folded her arms over her chest and frowned harder.

"That happens when you're a kid too, Ellie." Parker stared at her sister pointedly.

"It's true," their dad said. "But I think what Ellie's getting at is that sometimes you have to do things you don't want to do as you get older. Handle more responsibility, even if it isn't fun. And to answer your question, L-Bean, it's time because your aunt and uncle think it is. And I happen to agree. You're mature enough now to learn the value of a sacrifice."

"Happy birthday to us." Parker let out a dramatic sigh. "I still don't understand why I can't go to CUT while you're away. It's the perfect solution. It's a whole supervised sleep-away camp! You won't even have to worry about me. Ellie likes old people. She can hang out with them in Harborville while Clara and I are away. She'll be fine. Right, Ellie?"

Ellie looked sour.

"I'd rather you be here too," she said to her sister.

"Well actually . . ." Their dad cleared his throat. "There's another part of it—"

Just then, the waitress came over to the table.

"How are we doing?" she wanted to know. "Need any boxes?"

"No, thanks." Ellie said politely.

"No, thanks," Parker grumbled. Did Ellie not care? Was she not angry? Of course she wasn't. *She* didn't have Clara and CUT. *She* could just do whatever she usually did in the summer, like talk at her fish and grow tomato plants in the backyard and transfer ants out of the kitchen on a piece of peanut-butter smudged loose-leaf paper. Why could she not be NORMAL?

When the waitress walked away, their dad looked different.

"The reason you can't go to CUT is that you aren't just getting to know George and Mabel here in Harborville," he told them, looking them each in the eye. "You're going to go with them to their farm up north, in the mountains. They have someone who looks after it when they're away, but apparently, they could use an extra couple of hands right now. It's the perfect opportunity for you to learn something new and live somewhere different and do some of the things your mom did as a kid. Haven helped her become who she was, and I happen to think she was pretty great. There is a lot more to the world than Harborville can offer you, or even that I can offer you by myself.

Besides," he said, attempting a joking tone, "it's time you got a little country to balance out the city slickers in you."

Suddenly Maggie's pancakes felt like a pile of rocks in Parker's stomach.

"I know it's sudden," Parker's father's voice sounded tired. "And it's not ideal. The good thing is, it's a week to summer vacation, so you won't miss much school."

"WHAT?" Parker shrieked. "We're supposed to go to this . . . *farm* . . . before we even finish the school year?"

"Tomorrow morning," her dad said.

Even Ellie looked like she might puke. "Why so soon?"

"It's when George and Mabel are able to come collect you," he said. "I'm sorry. I've already told your teachers, and—"

"Does everyone know about this except us?!" Parker's blood was now boiling, and she felt a strange tingling sensation all over. She tried to stay calm as the waitress dropped off their check.

"No," her dad said firmly. "George and Mabel just called me this morning." He slipped his credit card in the little black folder and handed it back to the waitress.

"But . . ." Ellie looked at her empty plate, as if the news has just settled into her stomach—like her breakfast for dinner.

"They're strangers," Parker finished.

"Well," Parker's father leaned forward. "That's a reason to look forward to this. You don't know your mom's family, and I know she wanted it for you. It's going to be strange and it's going to take getting used to . . ."

Ellie shuffled in her chair. "I guess eight weeks isn't so bad," she said.

Parker turned and stared at her sister. Ellie was studying her father's face like it was a menu.

"That's right." Her father shifted, somehow pulling the conversation to a close as he signed the bill and scooted his chair out from under the table. "Eight weeks is just a blip in the grand scheme of things."

Parker stood up, her feet sticking a little to the syrup on the floor. Somehow even after the four pancakes she'd managed to eat, she felt empty. But more than that, she felt *angry*. Just after they slipped through the door and began walking to their car, she understood why. It was CUT. But it was also more than CUT. She stopped in her tracks.

"Dad." He and Ellie turned around. Parker knew they weren't going to like what she was about to say. But that was growing up, right? Growing up meant facing things they didn't like; why not start now?

"Why do we have to do a thing Mom wanted us to do? She *disappeared*. She left us. You and Ellie just want to believe she died in the ocean because it's easier. But we don't know that.

The only thing we know is, she's *gone*. But we're all here acting like she still calls all the shots."

For a second, her dad's face flickered with frustration. Ellie looked like she was about to cry. Parker felt bad, as terrible as she'd felt when their mom went away in the first place. Then Ellie took their dad's hand, and his face softened. Now he just looked sad.

"Come here, Sweet P," he said to Parker, waving her closer. Parker stepped into his embrace, right there in the parking lot, relieved. She'd said the most horrible thing, but her dad was hugging her anyway. He wrapped his arms around both girls.

"Your mom loved you girls more than anything," he said. "But I think you'll understand that better if you learn more about her life. And Haven is the best place to do that."

After that, everything was sort of a blur.

Parker remembered climbing into the back of their blue SUV and buckling up.

She remembered getting a string of texts from Clara and texting a sad face emoji back.

She remembered sitting in her room and then going downstairs and grabbing her basketball from the hall closet and telling her dad she was going to shoot hoops at the community court.

"No more than an hour," her father said. "Back before dark."

Parker felt the cool night air against her burning cheeks. It was not comforting.

At the court, she stood on the three-point line, spinning the ball in her hands. Without thinking about it, Parker dug her fingers into the bumpy rubber of the ball. She thought about the summer that was about to unfold—a week early—and the summer she'd been dreaming of.

All that time! All that practice! And it all meant nothing! Why?!

She thought of her mom.

Parker squeezed the ball harder.

She hated what was happening to her. She hated that things were always just *happening* beyond her control. The world was always shifting out from under her feet, and there was nothing she could do about it. Other people had normal lives. It didn't seem like things were this hard for Clara.

Why Parker? Was she cursed? The heat she'd felt at Maggie's was coursing through her now, consuming her entire body. Even the air conditioner on the ride home hadn't helped.

She bounced the ball carefully. She looked up at the basket.

"Come on, Parker." She spun the ball in her hands. She bounced it again. Aimed. And tossed it at the basket. It connected with the headboard. Parker had been making baskets on this court since she was six. And now?

"What is wrong with me?" Parker whispered. She wiped sweat from her forehead with the back of her hand. Then she threw the ball again. This time the ball hit the board so hard, it almost cracked.

Parker tightened her fingers into fists. Anger coursed through her. Engulfed her. The ball rolled toward her feet. She went to kick it away and missed. She brought her foot down hard on the ground, like a stomp.

Like the stomp you do when everything is going wrong.

Her foot slammed down on the asphalt. Hard.

The ground cracked and jolted Parker out of her rage. For a second her whole body rattled like someone was shaking her.

When it finally stopped, Parker looked down. *Huh?*

There, clearly, beneath her sneaker, was a split in the ground. *Earthquake.*

"Parker?"

Parker spun around in time to see her father standing at the edge of the basketball court, looking like he'd just seen the earth crack in two beneath his daughter's feet.

CHAPTER SIX

Of course Ellie knew that people, like cats, squirrels, and fish, come in all shapes and sizes, but there was something about seeing two such different people standing next to each other that was very interesting. Ellie's great-aunt Mabel and great-uncle George were definitely very interesting.

For one, they showed up at six o'clock in the morning the day after Ellie and Parker's twelfth birthday. It happened to be a Saturday. This was not when people typically showed up, unless they had plans to watch the sunrise with you. Ellie had not even had time to pack, and she knew Parker had not packed either, other than maybe a getaway bag. Ellie would not have put it past her.

There were other unusual things about Mabel and George. For one, there was their knock on the door—they hadn't even touched the doorbell—and *what* a knock.

It was so big, Ellie thought it was a construction crew at the door. Or that it came from a giant from a fairy tale. It was so loud it practically bumped Ellie out of bed. She entertained the vague hope that it *was* a giant there to watch the sunrise.

"Parker?" She whispered. There was no answer from the top bunk. Ellie slid out of bed and confirmed that Parker was not there. For a second, she worried that Parker really had run away.

Ellie stepped out of their room and peered around the corner.

"Aunt Mabel and Uncle George are here!" Parker hollered. Ellie felt herself sag with relief. Parker had not gone anywhere.

Ellie walked to the top of the stairs. Sure enough, there they were, looking up the stairs at Ellie from two different vantage points.

"Hello, I'm your uncle George," one of them said, just loud enough for Ellie to hear. "But you can just call me George."

"Hello, George," Ellie called from the top of the stairs. "It's nice to meet you." Ellie could hear her dad bustling in the kitchen already and could smell the comforting aroma of fresh coffee. She thought about going downstairs, but something stopped her. She wanted to observe from afar, before all the typical things happened to paint a picture of someone.

Ellie could see from where George's head hit the level of the paintings on the wall that George was almost twice as tall as Ellie, probably even taller than Ellie's dad. George was fine-boned and willowy. His delicate features were framed by a cumulous cloud of silver hair. His eyes were a startling shade of turquoise blue, the kind of blue Ellie had seen in ads for cruise lines. The other relative (whom Ellie deduced was Aunt Mabel by process of elimination) was only a couple of inches taller than Ellie, which made her small for a grown-up. Mabel also had bright blue eyes, and she wore her black hair—streaked with two thick sections of white—in a bun on top of her head, which for some reason made her seem even shorter rather than taller. Her only accessory was a pair of bright red glasses with round frames.

Mabel looked, Ellie thought, like a really cool, bespectacled baby zebra. But Ellie did not say this out loud.

Both Mabel and George were wearing overalls—thick denim that seemed to be covered in pockets, and the kind of big rubber boots used for walking in something thick and muddy.

"Hello!" Mabel smiled as Ellie descended the stairs. "You must be Ellie! I'm your great-aunt Mabel! We're so pleased to see you again after so many years!"

Mabel's voice was booming and insistent but cordial. It was a voice that invited itself into a room, occupied all the furniture, and emptied out the fridge before leaving. Mabel's voice was way larger than Mabel.

"We were just telling Parker how wonderful it is that you're all grown up," George added. George's voice, on the other hand, was warm, smooth, and cozy. It was the kind of voice you hoped would read you a story.

"Twelve yesterday," Ellie confirmed. Out of the corner of her eye, she saw Parker scowling at her. *Traitor,* the scowl said.

"Girls, bring George and Mabel into the kitchen," her dad said. "I've got coffee and danishes here."

"That'll hit the spot," George said in a tone Ellie would expect a very tall tree to speak in if trees spoke. He set his bag down by the front door. "We've come a long way to collect you girls."

"Dad never gets up this early," Parker informed them accusingly. "He likes to sleep in."

"We're on Florida time," Mabel explained, as if that cleared everything up.

In the kitchen, Ellie's father was not only up, he was bustling around, trying to make George and Mabel comfortable. He'd even brought out Mom's fancy tea set in addition to a carafe of coffee, and there was a plate of danishes on the table. Ellie was a little hurt by this display. She looked at Parker, whose lips had formed a thin line.

"Funny how our birthday breakfast didn't happen," Parker mentioned coldly. Mabel and George tactfully pretended they hadn't heard.

"This is lovely," George said. "We took a redeye from

Florida and the train from the airport. We haven't even been back to Haven yet! It's so nice to be someplace familiar."

"But you haven't been here since we were babies," Parker pointed out. "How could it be familiar?"

"George simply meant it's comforting to gather with people we love!" Mabel explained loudly. "Especially after a long and arduous journey." Mabel added cream to her coffee and crossed the kitchen. She stood on her toes to get a better view through the back windows. Ellie straightened, hoping the garden beyond looked OK to Mabel; after all, she ran a whole farm. Ellie tried her best to keep everything healthy and cared for.

"Lovely!" Mabel exclaimed, and Ellie let out a sigh she hadn't realized she was holding. She joined Parker at the breakfast nook and made efforts not to stare at her new family. There was something about them. Not just their differences in size and manner, but also the ways they were the same—the same careful way they stirred their hot beverages. The way they both seemed perfectly comfortable being awake at a time when everyone else was still waking up.

"What were you doing in Florida?" Parker sounded suspicious.

"A little of this, a little of that!" Mabel said enthusiastically, if vaguely.

"That's right," George agreed, nodding then sipping his tea. Parker frowned.

"I hope you like danishes," their father interrupted before Parker could ask any more questions. To Ellie he seemed unusually nervous. "Or pancakes? We just had pancakes, though. How are you all for donuts?"

"Danishes are perfect." George selected one from the proffered plate and took a bite. "Mmmm," he said. Ellie's dad looked relieved.

"I've eaten," Mabel bellowed. "But it was kind of you to think of us."

"It was no trouble." Ellie's dad was fidgeting in a way she'd never seen. Maybe it was because he wasn't used to being around someone taller than he was, Ellie speculated. "Well . . ."

"No time to dally," Mabel broke in. "Girls, are you all packed?"

"What?" Parker's jaw dropped.

"We're leaving . . . *now*?" Ellie asked.

"Why, yes," George told them. "We've only got forty-five minutes till the train leaves. That's it for today! Not too many direct trains to Bearsted. That's the town up north that Haven is in."

Ellie looked at her dad. Even he looked surprised.

"Well now, there's no rush," he said. "I thought you could spend some time here for a night, ease the transition . . ."

"I'm afraid there *is* a rush," Mabel broke in. "It's actually rather urgent that we reach Haven today." She met Ellie's dad's gaze with her own, and it was as though their pupils were wielding tiny dueling swords. Her dad backed down first.

"OK," he agreed. "In that case"—he fiddled around in his pants pocket—"I've been holding on to this for the two of you." He drew out Mom's bracelet—the one that had been discovered after her death. "I'd like to give this to you," he said to George and Mabel. "I know you had asked after it and . . . well, I couldn't bear to part with it before. But it seems like now is the right time, since you'll be watching after our girls. Ginny would have wanted you to have it."

"Really, Dad?" Ellie was astonished. She had always assumed the bracelet would one day belong to her and Parker.

"Yes," her dad said firmly. "George and Mabel gave your mom this bracelet when she first went to Haven as a girl. It's only right."

Mabel reached out to accept the bracelet. "Thank you," she said. "We'll treasure it."

Ellie's dad nodded. "Now, girls, go pack your bags. Drawing out a goodbye will only make it harder."

"Are you KIDDING?" Parker stood up, forgetting the bracelet. "What about Clara? What about all my friends? I can't even say goodbye?"

"I'm sorry, but no," George said. "It's regrettable, but everything is happening very quickly."

"What is happening?" Ellie asked, curious.

"You'll see when we arrive," George said. "We really must be off. We aren't morning people, really. We would have come later if there'd been time to dawdle."

Ellie was mystified. What could possibly be so urgent at the farm? And why were they so adept at impersonating morning people?

"I cannot believe this," Parker said. "I'm not going." She leaned back in the nook and folded her arms across her chest. Her cheeks were a deep red, almost purple. Ellie felt bad for her sister. She did not take change very well, and Ellie could tell she was about to cry.

"Parker, go pack your bag, *now,*" their dad said.

Both Ellie and Parker's jaws dropped. He never raised his voice with them. Parker's eyes spilled over, and she ran up the stairs. Ellie followed her, pausing only briefly at the kitchen threshold.

"Can I bring my fish?" she asked in a small voice. The thought of leaving Walter behind was too much to bear. "And my plants? Who will look after my plants?"

"Of course," George assured her. George's eyes were very kind, Ellie noticed. "Whatever you can carry. You won't need much else."

"Why not?" Ellie wanted to know. Her heart pounded at the thought of all the things she wanted to bring that maybe she could not.

"We do things a little differently at Haven," George explained. "Pack your very favorite things, and don't worry about practicalities."

It was a strange directive, Ellie thought, as she followed Parker upstairs to their room. What if her favorite thing was bubble gum? Should she pack a bag full of bubble gum? Luckily, she detested chewing bubble gum because it felt like a task perpetually unfinished. She had already mentioned two of her favorite things—her plants and Walter. Her other favorite things were her gifts from her mom. That was everything important that belonged to Ellie.

"I don't want to go to a weird place with these weird people," Parker was muttering, as she began sorting through her belongings. "I can't believe I don't even get to say goodbye to Clara."

"That does seem unfair," Ellie agreed. She felt Parker's eyes on her, and knew it was because they rarely saw eye to eye. "What?" she said. "It does. It would be like me having to leave without saying goodbye to Walter."

"Ugh, that is not even the same thing at all." Parker shook her head, annoyed. "Clara is a *person*. She is my *friend*."

"People can have friendships with animals too," Ellie pointed out. "People can love animals just as much as humans, in fact. Maybe *more*."

"Are you speaking from experience?" Parker wanted to know.

Ellie didn't say anything. Secretly, she felt saying goodbye to Walter would be much harder than saying goodbye to Clara, but she didn't want to argue.

"I still don't understand why they never visited us till now," Parker was saying.

"You heard Dad. They've always been far-flung. I feel bad for them," Ellie reflected. "It would be hard to be flung far from home."

"Ellie." Parker whirled around to face her, her hands on her hips. "That is *exactly* what is happening to us. Except it's worse because we aren't choosing to be flung."

"Oh," Ellie said. Her sister had a point.

Parker poked her head back in her closet, and Ellie began to carefully wrap the gifts her mom had given her over the years: a broken compass, an astrolabe, a whistle. All of them were precious to Ellie; she would have to collect the weather vanes from the backyard too. Ellie snuck a look at Parker, whose legs were sticking out of the bottom of her closet where she was kneeling on a pile of dirty laundry and sorting through footwear.

Ellie did not like deceiving her sister. But she felt this was one of those rare moments where maybe the deception was worth the payoff. Ellie quickly moved across the room to Parker's own set of drawers, which (thankfully) were already open. She rummaged around, heart thudding, until she found the box that contained Parker's silver bracelet buried under a stack of underwear (ick). Ellie carefully rearranged the underwear (double ick) and slipped the bracelet into the pocket of Parker's favorite tie-dyed windbreaker just as Parker emerged from her closet, looking stressed.

"Do you think we'll need our roller skates?" she wanted to know. She stuffed a thick binder full of stickers into her bag.

"I don't think so," Ellie replied, trying not to look guilty. "I doubt there's much pavement on the farm."

She knew Parker would leave the Harborville house without even noticing her gift from Mom was missing from her bureau. But Ellie had the distinct feeling that the gifts would be more important to Parker someday than she realized in this moment. And Ellie wanted to be prepared for when that day came.

CHAPTER SEVEN

Technically, Parker knew the world was always moving at the same speed.

Time was a constant. Which meant that the space between seconds, minutes, hours was always the same. Like how a mile was a mile and a yard was a yard. When Parker was playing sports or even just running fast, she could feel the seconds beneath her sneakers; she could see them in the air. She could always tell at the end of a lap if she'd gone faster or slower than the last time. When Parker was running, or playing, it was like she owned time. Like she could use it, fill it up with steps.

But now it felt like time was slipping through her fingers.

One moment they were sitting having pancakes for dinner, the next, there were two strange people in overalls showing up at the front door to participate in their dad's abandonment. Parker wanted time to stop; she wanted to stay where she was. But it was as if everything was flowing around and away from her. Before she could say anything about it, she was standing in her bedroom with a suitcase on her bed and all her clothes and her sticker album stuffed inside. At the last minute, she remembered to grab her journal from beneath the stack of novels on the shelf by her bed.

While Ellie fussed over Walter, Parker texted with Clara, who was for some reason awake.

Clara: I can't believe you're going TODAY.

Parker: Me neither

Clara: What if they give your CUT spot to Reagan Merkin???

Parker: 🧝

Clara: Do farms have WIFI????

Parker: 😭

Standing over her suitcase, Parker felt hot again, like she might even faint. Ellie was still preoccupied by Walter—murmuring something to him again. Parker sank onto the end of Ellie's bed. The list of things in her life that were changing was so long that she had had to stop listing them in her journal because it was too depressing.

No going to school for the last week, which was always a fun celebration more than actual school.

No more seeing Clara every day.

No more chance at CUT.

No more Ultimate at all.

No burgers with her friends.

No more Dad.

> **Clara:** Is there an Ultimate team where you're going?

> **Parker:** I DON'T EVEN KNOW!!!

> **Clara:** 😭😭

Parker could hear Ellie humming while she bundled up Walter and gathered her succulents.

> **Clara:** Call me as SOON as you get there

Soon Parker found herself squashed in the back of their dad's SUV next to Ellie and just behind Mabel and George.

They both smelled faintly of garlic and earth and had chosen to sit side-by-side instead of one of them sitting up front with Parker and Ellie's dad. Weird.

Parker's dad hugged her and Ellie at the train station. "Make me proud," he said.

He looked like he was about to cry, so Parker held back all the things that were on her mind. Instead, she said, "I love you." And then they stepped aboard the train which, despite everything, was sort of cool.

The journey took six hours, and Parker slept the entire time. When she woke up, the train was pulling into the station and Ellie was nudging her from the seat next to her.

"We're here," Ellie whispered, sounding excited for some reason. "Wake up!"

"I was hoping this was all a bad dream," Parker muttered. But she picked up her duffel and followed Ellie, George, and Mabel toward the front of the train when the conductor announced, "Bearsted Station."

"Ellie, look," Parker whispered, nudging her sister as they followed their aunts and moved past all the other passengers who were getting off at later stops. Casey and Cassie Phillips—a.k.a. the Twins—were seated next to each other three rows up. Casey caught Parker staring and gave her a friendly smile. It was like being recognized by a celebrity.

Parker waved back, a little disappointed when Casey and Cassie didn't stand up to exit at Bearsted.

"How do you know him?" Ellie asked.

"He's really good at sports," Parker told her sister. "So is Cassie. Cassie has set a school record at, like, everything. *Everyone* knows them. The question is, how does he know me?"

"Maybe he was just being friendly," Ellie suggested, shrugging. Parker followed her sister, George, and Mabel in stepping off the train onto a step stool below. On the platform, she looked around. There was a river just beyond the tracks. Ellie was turning around and around, *ooh*ing and *ahh*ing at the mountains that surround them on all sides like hulking beasts. Ellie didn't seem to mind so much that they'd left Harborville.

"How will we get to Haven?" Parker asked, following George and Mabel, who were walking swiftly toward the exit. She craned her neck for other signs of life, but it seemed they were the only passengers getting off at Bearsted. That was *not* a good sign.

"We had a friend drop off our car," Mabel explained. "His name is Ray. He and his grandson, Felix, tend to Haven when we're gone." She held open the doors to the station and ushered the girls inside, then through the lobby and back out again, where they spilled into a small parking lot. Parker scanned the meager smattering of cars, wondering which belonged to Aunt Mabel and George.

"Come on, then." Mabel led them to a large, dusty pickup truck. She picked up Ellie's suitcase and placed it in the back, then reached for Parker's. "This is us," she said, stating the obvious.

Parker slid into the narrow back seat next to Ellie, who looked positively delighted.

"I like your truck," Ellie said. "It's very truck-y. I've never been in a truck till now."

"Family antique," George told her, twisting the key so the truck rumbled to life. "Hope it makes it to Haven!" George twisted around and gave the girls an ominous wink.

Driving on a bumpy road in a pickup truck with two old relatives who were virtual strangers and a twin sister who couldn't stop talking was not Parker's idea of a good time. Every turn was like the ground underneath them was going from road to rubble to rock. Every inch was a little bumpier than the last, until Parker started to wonder if her teeth were going to crack to pieces and fly out of her skull. They passed a gas station and a market on the way out of the station before turning onto a long, rural road. They went higher into the mountains on twisty, winding roads until Parker felt her ears pop. Every five minutes, Parker checked her phone and saw an empty space where her phone signal should be.

She was officially far from home and completely disconnected.

Finally, after what seemed like hours, George turned the truck in to a narrow driveway bordered by a low stone wall on both sides. Wild, untamed bushes rose up beyond the wall, obscuring the view of the property. Then they were bouncing and jolting their way up the drive until the truck ground to a halt on a patch of gravel.

George put the truck in park, and Mabel uttered her first full sentence since they'd begun driving: "Here we are!" she boomed.

George and Mabel opened the car doors and popped out, strangely lithe for how ancient they were. Parker slid out the back. The afternoon sun was high, illuminating all of Haven. Ellie gasped, shielding her eyes against the light that flooded the landscape of their new home.

But Parker's eyes were trained on the farm, which was not a farm at all, or at least not the kind of farm Parker was used to seeing in movies and books.

"Well? What do you think?" Mabel asked proudly.

George stood between Parker and Ellie and rested a palm on each of their shoulders.

"Welcome to Haven," he said, the warmth of his smile matching the sun.

Ellie looked at Parker, wide-eyed. For once, Parker was speechless.

Haven was *not* what she'd expected.

PART II:

THE DANGER

CHAPTER EIGHT

In the hours they'd spent on the train, Ellie had been witness to a variety of landscapes. They'd left the California coast behind and moved inland, past lush green slopes; sparkling rivers; endless rows of beige-colored stalks; and towering pine trees standing sentinel on snow-covered peaks. It had all served to paint an image in her mind of what Haven would look like. That is to say, these landscapes were beautiful but not surprising; she thought Haven would be the same—a *farm* farm, covered in hay bales and traversed by cows, perhaps with a red barn and a traditional, clapboard farmhouse. Ellie really hoped there would be a farmhouse. In the city, they lived in a remodeled rowhouse just like the ones on their right and left. She had never lived in a house with *character* and *stories*.

The farm they arrived at in Mabel's truck was not a typical farm, and it didn't even have a traditional farmhouse. Ellie wasn't sure it technically *was* a farm. All she could see was a very strange structure that seemed to defy gravity, plopped in the middle of a giant patch of dirt.

Parker wasn't sure what to make of it either, from the look of her. She was standing next to George, mouth agape, cheeks flushed like they did when she felt startled, angry, or embarrassed. Mabel was striding ahead to the farmhouse—if you could even call it that.

"I'll unlock the place and put on some lunch," she called back.

"Excuse me, George?" Ellie tugged on her uncle's sleeve, and George looked down at her. "What kind of farm is this?"

"Farm?" George let out a laugh. "Haven isn't a farm. Who told you it was a farm? Your dad?"

Ellie nodded.

"Well, I suppose I can see why he'd get confused," George said. "He's never been to Haven, and it's a bit difficult to sum up. There are certainly elements Haven shares with farms. We often have animals, and we grow some herbs and vegetables here."

"What would you call it, then, if it isn't a farm?" Parker had found her voice.

George paused, considering. "It's a sanctuary," he said. "But not just for animals. For all kinds of living things. For you and your sister too, if you let it. We don't use Haven for profit. When we're here, we work in service of the earth and

Haven's inhabitants. We consider Haven our ally, not our property. Haven gives us protection, and we give back by nurturing whatever grows and lives here."

"Well, we don't need a sanctuary," Parker grumbled. "We were just fine in Harborville." Parker stared at the farm that was technically not a farm like she wanted to sink into a hole in the ground.

"I'm sure you were," George said absently.

Ellie was wondering what George and Mabel needed protection from when a series of loud barks rang out, and a creature bounded toward them. "Oh! Arlo!" George exclaimed. The creature—which turned out to be a dog—jumped all over George and wriggled around ecstatically in the dirt at his feet before offering him its paw. George petted the dog for a while, paying close attention to his ears and haunches. When Arlo was finally calm and sitting on his haunches, he turned to consider Ellie.

Ellie sucked in a breath. She had always wanted a dog, but their dad had allergies. *This* dog was lovely. His fur shone a rich gray, nearly blue. He was medium size, with a sturdy frame. Seated, he came up to Ellie's knees. He had two black patches framing his eyes, and his sweet triangular ears were cocked over his head. His eyes held a depth of emotion and intelligence—even more so than Walter's. *Much* more so, if Ellie was honest (though it felt like a betrayal to Walter).

"Arlo, meet Ellie and Parker," George said, scratching the dog behind his ears again. "Arlo works here," he informed the girls. "He's a blue heeler."

Arlo offered Ellie a paw. She shifted Walter's bowl to her left hand and shook with her right, laughing delightedly. Then Arlo turned to Parker, extending a paw to her as well. Parker accepted it, seeming dazed; even she couldn't resist a smile.

"What do you mean, 'Arlo works here'?" Parker asked.

"Arlo is a cattle dog. He herds all kinds of animals—he's happiest when he's doing a job. We'll tell you all about Haven once you're settled," George said, scanning the grounds. "First, let's put your things inside Haven House."

"Can Arlo come?" Ellie was officially in love.

"Of course! We let all our animals inside the house if they would like to come," George replied. "Some animals prefer the outdoors. Arlo comes and goes. Arlo, would you like to come in?" Arlo barked twice and jumped high in the air.

Yes, Ellie could feel him say.

She looked at him, startled. It wasn't like he had actually spoken, but a strong *feeling* of "yes" had come out of nowhere. Weird. She didn't have time to pause and think about it, though. As they drew closer to Haven House, the rambling structure that had struck her as unusual from afar looked even *more* unusual up close.

"I can't believe I'm missing CUT to live in an actual junk-yard all summer," Parker whispered to Ellie as they climbed the front stairs to the porch.

"Shh!" Ellie jabbed her in the side with her elbow.

"Ow!" Parker shouted. Then, with genuine curiosity, she asked, "Is that wall made of doors?" She pointed at a second-story enclosure that seemed to be cobbled together with salvaged doors.

"Yes," George said. "I'm partial to the blue door with the brass mail slot."

The whole house—all four, staggered floors of it and what appeared to be a rooftop garden—was made from salvaged goods, as far as Ellie could tell. The roof on the first level looked like the kind of metal you might find on the side of an airplane; and in fact, Ellie could make out the first part of the words air fr— before it was cut off by another panel. The floor they were standing on felt like cobblestones but was actually the bottoms of blue and green glass bottles. A *lot* of the walls seemed to be made from doors bound together with clay. Some of the doors had cat or dog hatches built in. And no two windows matched—some were stained glass like the kind you might see at a church, some were the kind you open out to the world like in that first scene from *Beauty and the Beast*, some were floor to ceiling.

The four levels of the house weren't stacked neatly one on top of the other like most houses; they jutted from the sides with some overlap, which gave the house the look of a big LEGO tower or a living thing with arms. Ellie didn't think Haven House was a junkyard. Ellie thought it was magic.

"Well, come on in!" A warm voice emerged from inside the house. Mabel threw open the door, then came toward them, drying her hands on a rag and grinning from ear to ear. "You're here!"

"Hello!" Ellie waved. Even though they had just seen Mabel a minute ago, it was nice to be welcomed inside by a friendly face.

George stepped aside so the girls could go in first. Ellie noticed that Arlo was sticking by her side like Velcro. When she paused at the threshold to the house, he nudged her ankle with his cold nose.

Go, she felt inside her. Weird. She shook her head and stepped inside.

"Well, things aren't as dire as Ray and Felix led us to believe," Mabel said to George.

"He said some folks stopped by to help out in the spring," George agreed. "It always perks up when visitors arrive," he added.

"The right kind of visitors," Mabel amended.

"The kind visitors."

"Mmhmm. We'll have a better sense of things tomorrow."

"Let's get you girls settled," George suggested, grabbing Ellie's bag and leading them up a flight of stairs (made from mismatched stones).

Inside, the house was bright with the afternoon sun, and toasty, probably because of all the light streaming in the windows. Parker opened her mouth.

"We don't have AC," George explained, and Parker shut it again. "It gets chilly here at night, and we open the windows for a cross breeze during the day." Mabel had clearly been cleaning up, leaving a hint of lemon oil lingering in the air. There was a bowl of eggs on the table and another bowl with peaches. Ellie wondered how she'd done all that so quickly.

"Ray Findley, that friend of ours who looks after the place from time to time with the help of his grandson," George explained, ducking in order to avoid hitting his head as they made their way up the stairs. "He always sets us up with a few provisions to tide us over until we're on our feet."

Ellie's stomach grumbled.

George winked. "We'll get you in your rooms and then we'll have a proper lunch. Arlo, help Mabel make lunch." Arlo barked twice. "He likes having a job at all times," he explained. "Otherwise he gets restless and chews things.

Don't leave your toothbrushes lying around!" He laughed like he was kidding, but Ellie wasn't sure.

The stairs up from the kitchen were steep and narrow and seemingly endless. Ellie had to balance carefully to avoid losing her grip on Walter's bowl, which contained Walter's bag, which contained Walter.

"There are four bedrooms. Aunt Mabel and I are at the back on the left and right," George said, once they'd hit the top of the stairs. He reached for a door on the left, which looked like it had once been belonged to a bank vault. He had to twist an iron circle at its center in order to swing it open. "This is the first guest room."

It had a large bed up against one wall, facing a bay window. The walls were devoid of art, but they were painted a soft, muted green. Ellie noted that the room's soaring ceilings made it feel airy, and a sweet smell drifted from its source: a bunch of lilacs in a Mason jar placed on an upright log next to the bed.

"I'll take this one," Parker offered, pushing her suitcase through the door past Ellie and George. "Thanks. Oh, and what's the Wi-Fi here?"

George paused. "We don't have Wi-Fi here. We live pretty simply. All those extra signals complicate matters."

"WHAT?" Parker looked horrified, and Ellie cringed at her sister's reaction. "You don't—but how—"

"We have a landline for you to use to call your dad," George explained calmly. "If you'd like to send an email, I believe the Internet is available at the town library."

Ellie braced herself for a Category 5 storm. Instead, Parker slumped onto the bed, looking defeated. Without her apps she was totally cut off. Only old people sent emails; even Ellie knew that.

"Ellie will stay just across the hall, then," George said. "We'll be right back." Ellie stepped into the hallway behind George.

"I don't see any other door," she commented. She scanned the hall, confused. Then George pressed his hand on a panel in the built-in bookcase, and it swung open. Ellie gasped. A hidden door!

George smiled. "Your mom always liked that effect too," he told Ellie. "Just like magic. This room was always her first choice when she was here."

"Oh!" Ellie gasped when she saw the room's interior, then she set Walter's bowl and her duffel on the floor just inside the door. She clapped her hands. It was wonderful to imagine her mom standing in the exact spot Ellie now occupied, nearly twenty-five years prior. And her own room! She'd never had a space all her own.

"Most of the house is made from discarded bits and bobs," George went on. "I'm sure you've noticed. I believe the younger generation calls it upcycling. Mabel and I didn't build the house, but we've added to it. Every generation since it was built has added to it some way."

" 'Bits and bobs.' " Ellie laughed. "I like that. How did my mom add to it?"

"She and—" George paused. "Your mom added the rainwater trough on the ground floor, outside the kitchen. You wouldn't have seen it on your way in. It filters rain from the roofs and gutters into a container that we can use for washing clothes, flushing the toilet, and watering plants."

"Wow." Ellie felt her eyes widen. "I never would have thought of that."

"You'd be surprised what you can think of without so many distractions," George commented. Ellie assumed she was referring to the Internet, which she personally wouldn't miss, but she knew Parker would.

"Oh," George added, "we had some overalls made for you girls. They're hanging in the closets."

"Thanks." Ellie hesitated, not wanting to seem ungrateful. "Is it OK if we wear our regular clothes around the farm?"

"Of course," George told her. "But you'll probably find you'll want to wear the overalls. Your regular clothes will get ruined. Plus they're comfy! Like wearing pajamas."

Ellie approached the closet doubtfully and slid open its door. There was not one, but *five* pairs of overalls hanging on hooks, and a stack of white T-shirts folded on an adjacent shelf. Ellie pulled one of the hangers off the rack and inspected her new look. It actually wasn't bad. A soft denim in a shade of pale blue, it had a sweet little lion next to a little circle with a cross through it, both embroidered in red thread atop the breast pocket.

"Hey," Ellie said, recognizing the symbols. "I've seen these before! They're on the weather vanes my mom gave us for our birthday one year. Well, she left them for us—it was after she passed."

"She must have gotten those from Haven." George smiled. "The lion and earth symbol come from the Power family crest. Your mom always was sentimental."

"Really?" Ellie looked at her curiously. "That makes sense, then. The weather vanes don't do anything, so I figured they were decorations. They sat in our yard in Harborville and never turned at all, not even in the wind."

"Are you sure they don't work?"

"I can show you. I have them in my bag."

George nodded approvingly. "Smart girl."

Ellie returned the overalls to the closet, unzipped her duffel, and pulled out the small weather vanes. She'd wrapped them in old T-shirts, and she freed them carefully.

"Ah, yes," George said, peering at them with interest. "These do look familiar. I'm sure we used to have some like this around here. Why don't you put them out back and see what happens? Remember, no gift is without purpose. At least none your mom ever gave."

"Really?" Ellie stared. "Do you mean they might work, then?"

"Yes," George said. "But possibly not in the way you *think* they're supposed to work. Try to keep an open mind and see if they're trying to tell you something. A bad habit we human beings tend to have is closing off our minds to the unexpected. We dismiss things we don't understand. Just because we've been told something ought to work one way doesn't mean it's broken if it works an entirely different way. A lot of the time, we'd see and hear so much more if we only let ourselves."

Listen.

Ellie placed the metal objects on the bed and circled the room, running her hand over a wall made entirely of buttons. This room was smaller than the other one, but it was also cozy. It had a white iron bed with a pink comforter and blue pillows placed under a set of tall windows. It also had a sky-light, Ellie noticed with pleasure. She could look at the stars at night from bed! And there was a small wooden desk in the corner—perfect for Walter's bowl. The far wall was decorated with a world map, faded and covered in pin holes. Ellie felt a little tingle on the back of her neck. She was surrounded by things her mother had once touched and cared for. She had worried about the possibility of feeling homesick at Haven, but in that moment she felt the opposite: positively wrapped up in home. Parker poked her head around the door. She was already wearing her overalls.

"If I have to wear these, no pictures allowed," she said grumpily. "No one back home can see me dressed like this!"

Ellie laughed as Parker did an overexaggerated walk around the room. She looked like a paper doll shuffling across the floor, and her overall-clad thighs made a not necessarily pleasing *vvvt-vvvt* noise.

"You'll learn to love them." George smiled.

Parker looked dubious. But at least for the time being, she seemed to have temporarily forgotten about her digital inconveniences.

"I guess at least I won't ruin my city clothes," she agreed.

"Yeah! And check out all the pockets," Ellie said enthusiastically. Ellie was excited about all the cool stones and flowers and seeds she could keep in hers, but she figured Parker wouldn't mind having somewhere to stow that journal she was always carrying around as if no one noticed. "It's like we're a team!" Ellie added.

"Teams don't really wear matching overalls," Parker said.

"You don't know—" Ellie started, but before she had time to be hurt, Parker turned toward the map on the wall.

"Whoa! Cool. What's that funny list of numbers?"

Ellie looked at the bottom left-hand corner of the map, where Parker indicated. Her sister was right: What had looked like a map key at first glance was actually a handwritten list of numbers. Numbers their mom may have written herself.

"Coordinates, maybe?" she wondered aloud. "George, did Mom write these?"

"I'm not sure," George replied. "Maybe it's some sort of note your mom wrote to herself as a kid. She always liked things like that—secret languages, codes."

"Cool." Ellie looked at Parker, eyes wide. She hadn't known that. "This room was Mom's," she clarified for Parker's benefit.

"Oh." Parker's face closed off again, her eyes going flat. "I like my room better," she said. "It has superior windows."

"Well then. I'll leave you two to settle." George tucked some silver wisps of hair behind one ear. "You girls get comfortable. Bathroom's down the hall. Don't drink the water from the tap, it's not filtered. We use the bucket by the sink to flush the toilet. There's jars of filtered well water in the fridge. Come down for lunch whenever you're ready." Then he turned on one heel and was off, trailed by a faint whiff of lilacs.

Ellie placed Walter's bowl on the desk and emptied Walter's bag into the bowl, where he swam several exuberant laps. Then she flopped onto the bed, giving it a bounce. "You can come in whenever you want, if you want to be in Mom's room," she told Parker.

"I mean"—Parker turned around—"technically Dad's room at the house was Mom's room too. It's not like I haven't been in a 'mom room' before."

"This is different though," Ellie said. She touched the map. "It's old, but there's more of Mom here, because maybe she was our age when she was here." She hesitated. "Maybe we can finally find out what really happened to her," she suggested. Ellie knew in her heart that their mom hadn't abandoned them. But she thought some cold, hard proof might help Parker know it too.

Parker shrugged. "I'm hot," she said abruptly. "I'm going to put on something lighter. See you downstairs."

At least Walter was happy, Ellie observed. He was *very active.* He even did a little leap in his bowl, sending water splashing onto the desk. Ellie laughed. It was funny how Walter could be at home anywhere, as long as he had his bowl.

"Do you like your new view?" she asked him.

Oh yes, she felt.

She stepped back as if jolted. "Get it together, Ellie," she whispered. She knew she tended to talk to herself—and animals—without even realizing it. She figured it was a healthy way to keep herself company. But if she didn't stop talking to the fish, she might actually start thinking the fish was talking back. And then she would be on the wrong side of weird. The kind of weird that got people in trouble.

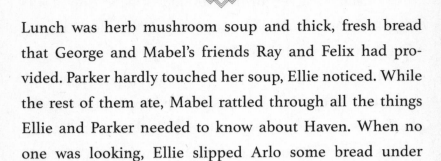

Lunch was herb mushroom soup and thick, fresh bread that George and Mabel's friends Ray and Felix had provided. Parker hardly touched her soup, Ellie noticed. While the rest of them ate, Mabel rattled through all the things Ellie and Parker needed to know about Haven. When no one was looking, Ellie slipped Arlo some bread under the table.

Thanks, she thought she heard Arlo say. *I'm not allowed table scraps, but I suppose one bite won't hurt.*

Ummm. Ellie snatched her hand back like it was on fire. It seemed her imagination had too much space to roam in the quiet of the country. Her head wasn't filled with the noises and distractions of Harborville, so she had to fill it herself. That was it.

"Arlo seems to like you," Mabel observed with a wink, before turning to watch Arlo chew. Ellie gave her a guilty smile.

"Does it feel any different at Haven than Harborville?" George asked, like she could read Ellie's mind.

"It feels more boring," Parker muttered.

"Parker!" Ellie gasped. "Dad would be so mad at you right now."

"Well Dad isn't here, is he?" Parker had been even colder ever since she'd heard about the Internet, but now her face was squished up in anger and red as the tomatoes in the bowl on the table. Ellie had never seen her so angry. "He abandoned us just like Mom did. So I guess I can do whatever I want now. And by the way, this mushroom soup tastes like barf."

Mabel calmly placed her knife and fork on her plate and gave Parker a measured look.

"I'm sorry," Ellie began. "We aren't usually so—"

But George held up a hand to silence her. "Do you really think your mother abandoned you, Parker? Oh dear." The sides of George's mouth were turned down, as if he'd tasted something rotten.

"It's OK," Mabel said. "This is a lot of change all at once, and there's no need to sort everything out today. Parker, I think you'll find Haven more interesting once we take a look around outside."

"I'll take a look by myself," Parker said, pushing her chair back from the table, hard. She grabbed her windbreaker from a peg next to the door before stalking out. Ellie shrank in her seat, torn between following her sister—who was clearly hurting—and being polite.

"Don't go beyond the stone walls," Mabel called after Parker.

"Will she be OK?" Ellie asked.

"Haven is perfectly safe," Mabel told her. "Especially in broad daylight."

"As long as you don't go beyond the stone walls," George added.

Ellie bit her lip. She thought she should probably run after Parker.

Let her go, someone—one of Mabel and George?—said, as she teetered between sitting and standing. *Sometimes people just need space to work out their feelings.*

"All right," Ellie agreed. She looked back at Mabel and George. Mabel was squinting her eyes at Ellie, and George wore another funny expression. George's face was extremely expressive, Ellie was realizing.

"Who are you talking to, dear?" George asked gently.

Ellie paled. She looked down at Arlo. Arlo looked back with his wide, earnest eyes. Then he placed a paw on her foot under the table. *It's me,* he said. And this time, Ellie was certain she wasn't imagining it.

CHAPTER NINE

No Wi-Fi. A toilet that worked with rainwater. (And *yes*, Parker was going to need further instructions to understand that one. Thanks for nothing, George.) A big, dusty, empty plot of land surrounded by a stone wall, a scorching sun, and nothing to do for miles, that she could see. How was this a sanctuary?! Who in their right mind would seek shelter here? How could their dad have abandoned them to two old crones who only had each other and a house-shaped pile of garbage?

Also, who knew what would happen in eight whole weeks back home? Would her friends even remember her? Would Clara become best friends with Nonie? Entire middle school empires rose and fell in half the time she'd be at Haven. It was like the whole world was conspiring against her. It was like a giant practical joke that wasn't funny. It was her worst nightmare.

Parker felt trapped.

She crossed the dusty expanse marking the rear of the house and spotted a paddock clinging to a tall barn that listed slightly to the left. The place was more of a ruin than a farm. It looked more like a farm in a fairy tale, at the point when the evil witch has taken over and covered the whole place in thorny branches and tumbleweeds because no one likes her.

The paddock fence was broken. The barn door hung on a single hinge. Weeds grew as tall as trees and gripped the sides of all the buildings and structures like they were holding on for dear life. There were no animals. No chickens or even wild birds. Just dirt and dead branches and more dirt.

Besides the ramshackle old barn, there was nothing else to look at beyond some more untamed brush to the east, and the snow-capped mountains and the thick of the forest that lay beyond Haven's stone wall to the north. Parker wasn't sure what she was supposed to see in Haven, but with every step she took, the ground felt dryer and more cracked. It seemed as if the earth beneath her feet had never produced a living thing, and in fact might have sucked the life from anything that touched it. In contrast, the trees beyond the stone wall were lush and varied, a study in shades of green. Parker tried not to focus on the mountains, which were so dramatic in their beauty they seemed menacing.

The sky darkened to match Parker's mood; by the time she reached the wall—nearly two soccer fields' length from the house—the cloud cover was heavy and threatening to burst. Parker hesitated, looking back toward the house. She'd half expected Ellie to follower her. But Ellie was so comfortable here already that it seemed she didn't need Parker anymore. Parker felt a deep fissure in that part of her heart that Ellie occupied.

She turned back to the wall. Mabel and George had said not to go beyond, but it was waist high and easy to scale with its jagged protrusions to grab onto. Parker was hot and exhausted in every which way, and the trees promised shade and maybe even water—she could hear the faint sound of trickling water.

And besides, it might be nice to make them worry. To make Ellie worry.

When people worried, you knew they cared.

It was an awful thought.

Parker hoisted herself over the wall by locking her feet in grooves between the stones until she was high enough to muscle her upper body above the wall's edge and swing her legs on top. Finally she was sitting on the in-between. Behind her was the house, a family she hardly knew, and a history she didn't want. In front of her was the promise of shade and the unknown. Parker leaned forward and let her body drop soundlessly to the other side, atop a bed of pine needles.

To her surprise, Parker had landed exactly at the foot of a path.

If the sky had been threatening on the other side, within the trees it may as well have been nightfall. Parker rustled in her left pocket for her phone and pressed the flashlight button. In doing so, her home screen lit up. Parker's jaw dropped. There, like a miracle on her worst day, was a single bar of phone reception.

Parker walked a little farther along the path, away from the house. Sure enough, soon there were two bars: Her signal was growing stronger the farther she was from Haven.

"Figures," she muttered. Parker took a sharp turn and followed the spindly path. The ground was no longer flat; it sloped gently, and then a little steeper, until she realized she was walking full-on into the mountains along some sort of hiking trail.

At a particularly steep point, she gripped the sharp edge of a gray boulder and heaved herself up. She reached past a tuft of grass and grabbed the next ledge, gritting her teeth against the pull of gravity. She would climb her way out of Haven, toward full-signal civilization. She would just keep putting one hand up and one hand up until Haven was just a pinprick behind her.

And then, just when she finally reached an overlook at the top of the incline, she felt a sudden, familiar but shocking sensation in her hip pocket. Her phone buzzed.

It freaked Parker out so much, she almost lost her footing. Her heart in her mouth, Parker yanked her phone out of her pocket.

A flurry of text messages filled the screen, rapidly downloading in a sudden flood of Clara. It looked like she had been messaging Parker every hour after she left. Lots of emojis and hearts and sad faces. Parker scrolled through the endless texts until she found the latest. There were some from a few hours ago.

Clara: HEY SOS CAN YOU LET ME KNOW YOUR ALIVE!

Clara: ANSWER ME PLS

Clara: CUT ORIENTATION WEEKEND IS SO AMAZING I WISH YOU WERE HERE

Clara: Ok it's weird you're not answering me

Clara: Where are u

Then there was a page of crying face emojis.

Then:

Clara: I GOT VOTED CAPTAIN!!!!!

Clara: MY ROOMIE IS SUPER COOL, HER NAME IS RAYNA

Clara: MAYBE YOU CAN COME VISIT ON A WEEKEND?? ILL ASK

Clara: GAH I ASKED THE COUNSELORS THEY SAID NO, WHAT A BUNCH OF JERKS I SHOULD WALK OUT RN

Clara: I'm SO SORRY

Clara: Parker?

Clara: I miss you I'm so sorry.

Parker sank down to the ground. She pulled her knees to her chest and looked around her. Through a gap in the trees she could see the sky roiling. She had never been anywhere this overwhelmingly *big,* this feral. An icy wind whipped around.

Parker was composing a text to Clara when the signal on her phone blinked away as mysteriously as it had appeared.

She balled her hands into fists and screamed. "GRAHHH!! STUPID HAVEN!"

She would just sit on this rock, she decided. She wouldn't go back to do chores or learn about Haven. Maybe not doing anything would cause a chain reaction and mess up the whole "farm." But Parker didn't really care.

This worked for several hours, because she fell asleep. It might have worked for more if Parker hadn't gotten intensely hungry.

According to her otherwise useless phone it was already seven. Seven o'clock and all she'd eaten all day was mushroom soup. And she'd climbed a mountain, and the rain had begun to leak through the foliage. Soon it would be dark for real—not just cloudy-dark.

Parker began to feel something she hadn't experienced in years, not since the night before they'd received the news about their mom.

She felt an instinctual pang of fear from deep within—an awareness in every fiber of her being that something bad was approaching. Heart pounding, she leapt to her feet and scrambled back down the slope, dirt coating her ankles and pebbles burrowing into her sneakers as she half ran, half slid toward Haven.

The incline was steeper than she remembered and though she knew she couldn't be far up the mountain, it was taking an eternity to get back down. The ground was wet and squishy. Parker struggled to keep her balance on the rocky parts, until, on a particularly steep incline, her heels slipped out from under her and she landed hard on her butt. As Parker pulled herself to her feet, blinking back tears, she felt a curious sense of déjà vu. But she had never been here before.

She moved forward along the path and then stopped. There were *two* paths to follow—a fork she hadn't seen before. *Fudge,* she thought, while fishing around in her back pocket for her iPhone. The screen was cracked from where she'd landed, and when she clicked on the Maps icon, nothing came up.

"UGHHHH," she screamed. The forest screamed back at her, but rather than being an echo, it was a growl.

The growl sounded like it was coming from all around her. Like it wasn't human *or* animal. Like it would eat Parker alive simply by surrounding her until she was absorbed into its nothingness. It wasn't an animal coming after Parker; *it was the forest itself.*

Parker picked herself up and ran.

She didn't know which path was the right one. She only knew they both led downhill, down toward safety, and if there was ever a time she believed Haven was a sanctuary, it was now. She ran until her lungs burned and big fat drops of rain smacked against her face. Thunder rolled just above as her sneakers made smacking sounds against the muddy ground. The rain slapped the stupid leaves of the stupid trees. Everything was tall and ugly and frightening, and Parker hated it all.

Mabel. George. Ellie. HAVEN. All of it.

In a flash, Parker's foot skidded on the mud a second time and she pitched forward, right into a stupid tree.

Face first.

Her whole body rang. She slipped down the tree to her knees, her fingers scraping bloody paths against the wet bark. Her head flooded with pain, grimy water seeped through the knees of her jeans, and something primal rose up within her, overtaking her body and mind. Parker shoved her cold fists into her jacket pockets. Her right hand folded around a strange object: a metal chain. She lifted it out and saw the silver bracelet her mother had given her for her birthday. She didn't take the time to wonder how it had gotten there. Instead, she clasped the bangle in her palm, opened her mouth wide, and released a howl that came from somewhere so deep, it was as if the howl was the whole of her. As it left her lips, Parker looked up, and her eyes filled with a blinding light.

The trees weren't burning, exactly; they were *glowing,* illuminated by Parker's palms, which were also glowing a deep shade of orange yellow. Parker screamed again, and the force of the blaze shooting from her palms nearly knocked her out. Something about gripping the bracelet tightly made her feel stronger. She pushed herself to her feet and ran from the accursed forest without bothering with caution.

After a while she saw dancing pinpricks of flashing light. The source wasn't her this time. She ran toward the light, and as she closed in on it, she heard voices shouting her name—above them all, Ellie's. When Parker finally reached the wall to Haven's edge, she screamed her sister's name with all her might, and three sets of arms reached over to pull her to safety.

What she never told them—not that night as she sat bundled by the fire sipping hot cocoa or any other time in the many years she lived after that—was that as they were tugging her arms toward Haven, she felt as if a million slender tendrils from the forest were fighting to pull her back and eat her alive.

CHAPTER TEN

Parker slept late the next morning. She slept all through breakfast and all through Ellie, George, and Mabel attacking the brush by the barn and all through the loud clanging sounds Ray made while patching the barn door and paddock fence. While Parker continued to sleep, they cleared branches out of the paddock. Collected and stacked firewood. Even cleaned out the barn, which was so full of cobwebs it looked like a haunted house.

Ellie said it felt like the spiders had more claim to the space than the people did, and she spent most of her time carefully transporting the spiders from the barn one by one in gentle hands, naming them as she went. "OK, Fred," she cooed, lowering her hand to the grass outside the barn. "See you later, old boy."

Parker's bank vault door stayed conspicuously closed till well past noon.

"Will she be OK?" Ellie nervously asked George and

Mabel at lunch, between bites of her cheese sandwich and peach pie.

"She will." But Mabel looked grim. "She's had a scare. She'll need to rest up, and then we should discuss a thing or two. This erratic weather is unusual for Haven, and we have a load of animals coming to stay today. We'll need to work together to keep things moving along and keep the animals calm."

"I see," Ellie said, though she felt a pang of anxiety shift from her heart to her stomach. Arlo felt it too. He placed a comforting paw on her foot, in the way she'd begun to love.

"Don't worry, Ginny dear," George said distractedly. "We'll get it sorted."

"Ellie," Ellie whispered.

"What was that?" George's head had been in the clouds ever since Parker had run off.

"You said Ginny, but she's Ellie," Mabel told her brother calmly. She placed a hand atop George's own. "Ginny is Ellie's mother."

"Oh goodness." George's brow furrowed from way up high. "I'm so sorry, Ellie. You just remind me so much of your sweet mother."

"It's OK," Ellie reassured him. "Lots of people think I look like my mom."

"The spitting image," Mabel said. Arlo flopped onto the floor and rested his head on Ellie's foot. Ellie wished she could ask him what's he'd heard about her mom, but she didn't want George and Mabel to be concerned about her newfound . . . habit.

"Can I help with the animals?" Ellie asked instead.

"You can watch," Mabel replied. "George will have to tend to them. Lots of the animals that come to us are sick or hurt, and Felix says we're getting at least a dozen today."

"Why so many?"

Mabel shrugged. "It's a bad time," she said. "There's got to be a balance to the way things work. If people take, they have to give back." She shook her head. "I know it's hard to understand at your age, but sometimes people act selfishly. That's where we come in. We try to reset the balance. Your mom did too. That was the focus of her environmental activism."

"What happens if the planet is imbalanced for a long time, with no one doing anything about it?" Ellie wanted to know. She was worried. If no one cared for living things, how could they all survive? She reached out to give Arlo a scratch behind the ears.

"Unfortunately, it wouldn't be good. The way we treat the earth really does matter," George said in a voice so wispy Ellie could almost see it, like steam from a mug of tea. "The earth is our home, and if we treat our home badly, we may lose it."

Ellie felt panic-stricken.

"We're not there yet," George reassured her. "But this year has been an especially hard one. Lot of crops dying, water supplies drying up. It's why we wanted you girls here to help."

"What can we do? We're only kids," Ellie pointed out.

"You can do much more than you realize," Mabel said. "But it's better if you discover for yourself how you can best contribute."

Ellie wondered if Mabel was aware Ellie could talk to both Arlo and Walter, and if so, whether there were other things she, Ellie, could do that most people couldn't. The thought made her pulse quicken.

"If this weather worsens, we'll be 'discovering' things from the shelter of the basement," George said softly. "Haven is usually such a peaceful place, Ellie. It's a respite from the rest of the world. If it's bad here, you can bet it's much worse elsewhere. If I'm not mistaken, that wind out there looks like an early sign of a tornado." Ellie stared at the wind whipping tree branches against the windows and thought of her dad, who was on his way to another continent by now.

"I think I'll put the weather vanes outside," she told Mabel and George. "Then maybe I'll give my dad a call."

"That sounds fine to me," George told her.

Mabel nodded. "When your sister is up, we'll show you around the sanctuary a bit, assuming the rain lets up."

"Usually Parker carries the sunshine with her," Ellie commented, before realizing how true it was. Their weather in Harborville was usually balmy and bright, and her sister had felt like a soaring comet every minute of every day. Last night she'd felt dulled and absent.

"That doesn't surprise me," Mabel commented, opening a gardening magazine as she sipped her coffee. "She's a force of nature, that one."

Ellie excused herself and took her plates to the sink, then ran upstairs to her mom's room. It didn't feel right to call it her own, because every single surface had evidence of Ginny Power written all over it. Mabel had explained that the button mural had started as a collection—Ginny had found them all in town before gluing them to her wall in the most unusual looping and swirling patterns. The quilt on Ellie's pink bed was also Ginny's, made from T-shirt scraps and a sewing machine. When Ellie sat on the bed and nestled into the quilt, she could see mountain peaks for miles outside her window. Ellie liked looking at the landscape and running her fingers over the little pieces of stitched-together T-shirts and imagining her mom collecting them thoughtfully. One from the ice cream shop, one from a skating rink, one with two pandas on the front, and one tie-dyed. Every piece had a story.

Ginny had even carved her initials in some of the wooden floorboards. Ellie was seated cross-legged on the ground and tracing one such board with her finger when it wiggled a bit. It was very loose, even for old, junkyard-scrap construction. Ellie pushed harder, and the board popped right out on the other end, like the high point of a teeter-totter. Ellie pulled the entire board off with both hands—it was only about two feet long—and peered into the space it left behind. There was a big hollow gap below, but it was dark and covered in cobwebs.

"Yuck," Ellie said aloud.

Yuck, agreed Walter, though he was just floating above his castle and couldn't see what she was doing from his vantage point. Arlo nosed around in the floor gap and sneezed, then emerged with a dust-covered snout.

Allergies, he told Ellie apologetically. He pawed at his nose and then licked it clean.

"It's OK," she told him. "But really, Arlo, you should practice better hygiene. You stay here and I'll get my flashlight."

When she shone the bright light from her phone into the empty space, Ellie saw a lot of things, not all of them pleasant.

She saw a mama spider and her babies scuttling away from the beam. She saw thick layers of dust and even a few dust bunnies, which were sort of cute, and the carcasses of dead beetles, which were not. She saw a wallet, and she saw a shoebox. She glanced at the door.

"Arlo, you keep watch," she told him, remembering he liked to have a job. "Bark once if someone's coming." The dog trotted obediently over to the door and flopped down in front of it. Then Ellie cracked open the wallet and peeked inside, heart pounding.

It contained fifty dollars and some change, which Ellie supposed was a lot of money back in her mom's day but was nonetheless disappointing as far as mysterious discoveries went.

Then she opened the lid to the box and gasped.

The box contained dozens of photos of her mother. Her mother laughing, her mother bent intently over a drawing, her mother as a kid in diapers, her mother as a teenager only a little older than Ellie. The photos brought tears to Ellie's eyes. Her dad had taken down all the photos of her mom after her death. "Too hard to look at," he'd said. "I just miss her too much." The only photo the girls had of their mother was the blurry one in profile in their Harborville bedroom.

So *this*—this treasure box—felt like a gift from the universe. Ellie sifted through the photos one by one, feeling only the tiniest bit guilty she hadn't waited for Parker. At the bottom of the box was a folded piece of paper, the kind with lines like she used in school, marked "Ginny." Ellie unfolded it. It was a drawing of two stick-figure girls standing on a mountain. They were surrounded by hearts and flowers, and they were holding hands with the sun shining down on them. One of them wore a pendent with a whistle at the end, like the whistle Ellie's mom had given both girls long ago.

"Love, Sadie," it was signed, with a funny symbol next to the name, like a set of parentheses with two lines going through it.

Sadie.

Ellie tried to remember her mom mentioning someone named Sadie, but she came up empty. Still, she felt like she was getting to know her mom better than she ever had when Mom had been alive. It felt wrong not to share it with Parker. She folded up the note and put it back in the box, then—on impulse—grabbed her own whistle, which hung from a plain metal chain, and slipped it over her head. She pressed her lips to it and blew. Nothing. Arlo didn't even stir. Oh well, at least it was a cute accessory.

Ellie packed the entire box back up and slipped it under her bed to show Parker later. Part of her wanted to dash over to Parker's room and show her *right that second,* but something held her back. After a whole night of not talking to Parker, Ellie had woken up feeling like something was wrong, and the feeling hadn't left her all breakfast, and if anything, now—alone in her room with her thoughts—it was worse, *especially* now that she had a secret she was keeping from her sister.

Normally after her Parker lost a game, Ellie felt bad. Somehow this *thing*—Parker breaking the house rules and nearly getting lost in the forest—felt way more intense. It felt like six bad games in one.

It felt really, really terrible.

Even Walter seemed anxious. He checked his bowl for missing pebbles and plastic seaweed and then gave the fish version of a shrug, which was subtle and hard to catch if you didn't know what you were looking for.

It's all here, Walter said, swimming in a little circle. *But it feels like something was misplaced.*

For the first time since she turned twelve, Ellie craved Parker's presence. That was it: *Parker* was misplaced. It felt like all of Haven was smothered, like a sandwich with too much peanut butter, without Parker as the silly and unpredictable jelly that gave it balance.

"What do I do?" Ellie asked, sitting in the desk chair in front of Walter's bowl.

What do you want to do? Walter asked. Arlo whined and settled himself on the braided rug at the foot of the bed. Ellie wasn't entirely clear on whether Arlo could understand Walter or vice versa, and she said so.

Some things, Walter told her. *Some fish things overlap with dog things. But my memory is very short, so it doesn't matter much to me either way.* Then he flopped onto his back and drifted for a moment, gazing at the ceiling.

"I just want to talk to my sister about what happened to her in the woods." Ellie frowned, tracing her finger around the glass of Walter's bowl. "Because something is definitely happening. Or something *happened*. Mabel and George are worried and lots of sick animals are coming in, and Parker hasn't talked since we found her last night. Why?"

One way to talk to people is to start a conversation, Walter offered. *You could do that. It worked with me and you.*

Ellie got up off the floor. "You're right. Thanks, Walter. Maybe Parker just needs me to ask." At that, she grabbed the weather vanes from the desk by Walter and resolved to ask her sister what the matter was the second she emerged from her room. It may have been her imagination, but it seemed like Walter waved a fin in her direction when she and Arlo left the room.

I don't know what the fish said, Arlo told her as they descended the stairs together, *but I think you ought to ask Parker what happened in the woods, and really listen.*

Ellie chose a clear patch of dirt to the left of the front porch to stake the weather vanes. She heard a truck rumbling up the drive and wondered if it was Felix with the animals. She took a look around and realized large tufts of grass had sprouted not just near the porch but also all over the field, which she could have sworn was just dirt and dust the day before.

Ellie frowned. She began walking toward the barn that lay on the outskirts of the property, Arlo at her heels. The barn was the only thing that made Haven feel like a farm at all, and it was hardly even visible from the long gravel driveway. As

Ellie walked, she noticed buttercups springing up around her feet, almost as if to mark her path. Funny. It really was much prettier in Haven today than it had looked on arrival.

"Arlo, did the rain do all this?" she asked.

Not the rain, Arlo said, then let out a joyful yip and scampered ahead, eager to run. If not the rain, then what? Ellie had to blink a few times to get rid of the notion that flowers were rising out of the earth *as she walked.* That was just impossible.

When she and Arlo reached the barn, she saw a bright blue pickup truck with a bunch of crates stacked in the back pulling a large silver trailer.

"Well, well, if it isn't Felix and Ray!" George was smiling and brushing the dirt off his knees as he rose from the fence he'd been tinkering with. "And Ellie! Great timing. I'd love for you to meet Felix especially—he's a few years older than you. Where's Parker?"

"Still in her room," Ellie said. George frowned and opened his mouth as if to ask another question, but Felix broke in.

"Long time no see!" he said to George. He was more than just a few years older than Ellie and Parker—sixteen, if Ellie had to guess—and almost as tall as George was, with short, sun-streaked hair, bright green eyes, and a smile that fit his large face and larger ears. He wore a red flannel shirt and a pair of dusty jeans with cowboy boots.

Ray hung back until Felix was done saying his hellos. "Hello, George," he said, giving Uncle George a shy smile. "Good to have you back."

To Ellie's surprise, George's normally pale cheeks turned a vivid shade of red, just like Parker's sometimes did. "Nice to see you too, Ray." George cleared his throat. "Ellie, this is Felix," he said. "And this is Ray. Felix and Ray: Ellie and her sister, Parker, are my late niece's daughters, and they're staying at Haven for the summer. Ellie, Felix and Ray do a terrific job looking after Haven when we're not here. They've also been the source of our bread and eggs and cheese."

"Thank you," Ellie said, shaking Ray's hand and then Felix's, which was as big as a pizza and twice as strong as any hand Ellie had ever shook. "The bread was yummy."

"Our pleasure." Felix smiled a toothy grin at Ellie. Then he turned back to George. "It's good to have you and Mabel back. This place is never the same without you here. And we've got piles of animals that need help. You came just in the nick of time."

"We came because Ray called us," George reminded him, glancing at Ray, who'd slipped away quietly and was stacking bales of hay in the front corner of the barn by the entrance. Taking his cue, Ellie crossed the barn floor to see if she could help. "Why so many?" George's voice was low, so low he probably thought Ellie couldn't hear him from where she stood.

"Pops says things aren't the way they used to be," Felix told George. His voice was grave. "It feels like something is off."

"Well." George cleared his throat and gave Ellie and Ray a significant glance. Then he inclined her chin toward the trailer. "Let's meet our newest guests."

"You got it. Pops, give me a hand." Ray and Felix strode over to the back of the trailer, pulled open the heavy metal door and dropped down a large ramp.

Ellie tilted her head, listening to the noises inside the trailer as Felix stepped inside. "Is it a horse?"

"Good guess," Felix called back from inside the trailer, which rocked as the first set of brown fuzzy legs appeared on the ramp.

Ellie felt like her brain was going to explode with happiness as the fuzziest creature she had ever seen in person emerged. Covered in caramel-colored fur, it looked like a teddy bear mixed with a bison. It had brown eyes and a soft pink nose. Felix turned the animal in a little circle. It was just about as big as the largest dog Ellie had ever seen.

Then she saw it.

Its left hind leg had a giant gash in it, almost as if the animal had gotten in a barn fight.

"The most urgent case is this guy. We've been calling him Toffee," Ray explained. "He's a highland cow. We found him tied to a fence at another farm a few miles outside Haven about a week ago. He's malnourished and has a nasty cut, already infected when we got to him. I think someone who couldn't afford him abandoned him, and then predators tried to get him and he couldn't defend himself very well, all tied up like that. We're worried he may not make it."

Toffee's head bobbed as he looked around. He looked frightened. Ellie winced, hoping Toffee hadn't understood Felix.

Ray passed Toffee's lead to George, who carefully walked Toffee into the paddock.

"I'll straighten you out in no time," George said to Toffee in a gentle tone. He ran two fingers up and down Toffee's nose, and Toffee's pained mewls quieted. "Has he been eating?"

"Hardly." Ray shook his head. "Seems like he's in a lot of pain."

"Do you think you can help?" Felix called from the trailer.

"I'll handle it," George said.

"Good, good." Felix slammed the trailer shut, startling Toffee enough that he skittered into George's leg and almost knocked him over. He stumbled maybe a little too easily, like George was already tired enough that he could be knocked over. Ray steadied him with a gentle hand.

"I'll take him," Ellie offered, reaching her hand out.

George passed her the lead with a smile. "Thanks. I'll be right with you."

"So. As I mentioned when we talked, we have a few sheep," Felix said, stepping toward the truck. "And some chickens, but their owner doesn't want them back. One sow. Oh, and a pretty cranky rooster with a bum wing, if you're fine with that."

"The more the merrier," George said. "I'm sure Toffee will feel better with some more company."

"We'll bring the sheep in while you tend to Toffee," Ray told him.

Ellie walked Toffee to the barn, careful not to pull or frighten him as he looked around with wide eyes. George had fixed up one of the stalls with soft fluffy wood shavings and a trough that Ellie filled up with water.

"Should I get him a blanket?" she asked George, watching as Toffee did a slow circle in his new space, limping a little and lifting his hooves when the shavings stuck to his fur.

"Cows aren't partial to blankets," George said, stepping up to Toffee and putting a gentle hand on his side. "The barn's plenty warm. He's just lonely and hurting, is all."

George knelt down so he was face-to-face with Toffee. "Got a bunch of company coming in a minute, so you won't be alone," he said.

His voice was warm and low, a soft rumble.

Toffee snuffled in response, almost as if he were fighting back tears.

"I'll treat him now," George told Ellie. "You're welcome to watch, if you'd like."

"Thank you," Ellie said, grateful George trusted her to be there. She watched intently as George rinsed the wound and applied an ointment. Then George put his hands on Toffee's injured leg and closed his eyes, leaving his hands in place. Two minutes went by, then three. Ellie fidgeted a little. When George finished whatever he was doing, he opened his eyes.

"Oh, this is healing wonderfully," George said, drawing Ellie's gaze down to the cow's leg. Toffee's skin had knitted together. The only evidence of what had been a raw, gaping wound was a pink seam from heel to hock.

"But how—"

"When you have a gift for it, all it takes is a little practice and a lot of understanding," George explained, looking into Ellie's eyes. "It's a rare and special person who can communicate with animals and know precisely what they need."

Ellie was silent, her mind whirring.

"Have you had that kind of experience, Ellie?" George asked gently.

Ellie hesitated. Then the events of that morning and the day before came tumbling out of her. When she was done talking, she almost didn't care whether George believed her or thought she was on the wrong side of weird. She felt so much better merely having told the truth.

"Oh, sweet child," George said, giving her a sad smile. "You don't ever have to pretend when you're at Haven. Things here aren't quite the same as elsewhere. You have nothing to hide."

"Really?" Ellie flushed with gratitude and wonder. "Can Mabel do it too?"

"No," George replied. "And neither can I—talk to animals, that is. But I can intuit where they're hurting and heal them more quickly than a vet can. You saw it for yourself. And Mabel has her own gifts. I'll let her tell you about those."

Ellie thought about it for a minute, and then nodded.

"Did my mom have a gift?" she asked.

"Your mom had several," George said. "She had more gifts than anyone I ever knew. Sometimes she was so connected to living things that it was painful for her." George paused, then opened his mouth again as if to say more.

Felix poked his head in the barn. "How's the patient?" he wanted to know.

"He'll be all right," George said. "He just needs to rest. Thanks, Felix." Then he nodded at the open barn door and the sun low in the sky. "It's got to be nearly two o'clock. Let's get your sister moving, Ellie. Sometimes hard work is the best medicine for a hard day."

It was true, Ellie thought. Having something to do was at least distracting. It was hard to think of anything else when you were exhausted. As soon as the sun came up that day,

Mabel and George had found one thing after another to do. They were always moving, digging, and pulling and pushing things around the land, which was starting to look a lot more like a sanctuary and less like a patch of sad earth.

On their way out of the barn, they passed Felix and Ray, who were attempting to corral a dozen sheep and chickens. Arlo immediately perked up.

"Arlo, help Felix and Ray," George said. Ellie couldn't make out Arlo's response because Arlo reacted with a giant garble of *yesyesyeshurrayhappydontmindifidoyesyaygetinlineyoulittlejerk*. Ellie raised her eyebrows, and George shrugged as the three of them watched Arlo expertly do his job, chasing the other animals and nipping gently at their heels until they formed an orderly line and marched into the paddock.

"Arlo loves herding," George said. "It makes him feel useful."

"He *is* useful," Felix replied. "That would have taken us hours." Then, faux-sternly, "Toffee had better be happy as a clam."

"A cow-clam," Ellie said. "Is that a cow in a shell? A cow-shaped clam?"

"Cut it out you two." George laughed. "He's just thrilled to be alive."

Ellie should have been happy, but all she could think about through afternoon tea with Mabel, George, Arlo, and Felix was Toffee. Every thought she had ended with Toffee's scared brown eyes.

"Ellie," Mabel said with a frown, rapping on the table as she held up a jug with the other hand. "I asked if you wanted lemonade rather than tea."

"Oh! Yes," Ellie said, holding up her cup. "Thank you." She drank her lemonade and ate her veggie quiche but couldn't get rid of that niggling feeling, no matter how hard she tried.

After tea and cleaning up the dishes, Ellie snuck back to the barn just to see if Toffee was OK. She found him standing in his stall where they'd left him.

"Hey, Toffee," Ellie whispered. "It's me, Ellie. I live here at the farm. I'm the girl who was here before. I wanted to make sure you're OK."

Toffee snuffed.

"I know George said you didn't want a blanket but . . . maybe you want more hay or something? Is your leg all better?"

Toffee snuffed again. This time louder.

Ellie paused. Instead of asking more questions, she listened.

After a moment, she heard a low, warbling voice.

Scared, Toffee snuffed. *Alone.*

"Oh!" Ellie rushed forward and put her arms around Toffee's neck. "It's OK! I'm here."

Toffee pushed his nose into Ellie's shoulder. *My leg.*

Ellie looked down as Toffee lifted his leg, still very pink and raw, off the ground. It hovered for a second before Toffee let it drop, grunting from the effort of raising it.

Suddenly the barn door creaked. Ellie looked up to see George standing in the doorway, holding a lantern to illuminate the dim space.

"Well then," George said. "Ellie, how's Toffee's leg doing?" His eyes narrowed with concern.

For the first time, Ellie spotted the glint of silver on George's right wrist, where his sleeve had slipped back as he held the lantern aloft. "He says his leg hurts," Ellie replied.

Then Toffee sank to the ground and let out a guttural moan. Ellie and George rushed over. Ellie gasped, bringing her hands to her mouth. Toffee's wound had reopened, and Toffee's eyes projected agony.

"This is not good," George said, looking alarmed. "Why didn't he heal? He should have healed completely. Ellie, he's in grave danger. I'll ask Ray to take him to the emergency vet tomorrow."

"But don't you usually do things the regular vets can't? That's your gift, isn't it?" Ellie struggled to keep her voice even. Seeing George's panic was making *her* feel anxious.

George nodded. It was the first time Ellie had seen her serene-seeming uncle look so upset. In the shadowy barn, his eyes looked big and his face drawn. "Yes, that's right. If I can't heal it, something is very wrong. I'll give him a tonic for the pain, and then let's go inside. I'm exhausted. Let's take it easy for the rest of the night and have a long talk in the morning. There are some things Mabel and I ought to tell you and your sister."

CHAPTER ELEVEN

After Mabel got back from town and Ellie and George got back from doing barn animal stuff with Felix, they all ate dinner. Everyone was strangely quiet. Even Ellie wasn't doing the weird thing where she muttered at Arlo.

Parker, of course, was wide awake, having slept exceptionally late. She was also extremely hungry, having skipped both lunch and afternoon tea. And she was restless from being cooped up inside all day (by choice). She shoveled down her food and shifted impatiently in her chair while the others took forever to finish. Once they'd cleared their plates and washed them in a big metal tub in the kitchen using rainwater (gross) and homemade lard soap (double gross), there was literally nothing to do but stare at the fire in the fireplace. Mabel settled herself in the heart of the living room while George stoked the fire.

"I want to talk to my dad," Parker said. "I want to call him. But I don't have a signal."

George looked confused. "Why would you need a signal when we've got the portable?"

"There's no signal around here, but there's a landline on the table just there," Mabel pointed with her teacup. "You can call on that."

"A landline?!" Parker gasped, walking over to the ancient beige brick in the corner of the room. The phone looked like an antique. She'd thought it was decorative.

"Cool," Ellie said with interest. "I've never called anyone on a landline."

Parker picked up the receiver and punched in the buttons for her father's number, which he had forced them both to memorize, although Parker had never had any reason to know it by heart until now.

"I want to talk to Dad when you're done," Ellie piped in.

Parker nodded. The line crackled for a few seconds before there was a click, then she heard her father's voice.

"Hello?" He sounded far away.

"Dad?" Parker asked. "Can you hear me?"

"Parker!" Her father sounded alarmed. "Sweetie! Are you OK? Is everything all right?"

"Yeah, yeah I'm fine," Parker said. "Ellie's fine too."

"Hi, Dad!" Ellie shouted.

Parker frowned, turning away so the others couldn't hear

her. "I wanted to ask you. I just . . . I don't want to stay here. I don't fit in. I want to stay with you, in Europe. OK?"

At first Parker thought her father had lost his connection. All she could hear was a spitting and popping sound. Like electric popcorn on the phone line. But then she heard a sigh. She could picture her father running his fingers through his hair, looking worried.

"Sweetie," her father's voice sounded strained. "I'm sorry, I just . . . I know it's hard being in a new place. The thing is, your aunt and uncle's place is the best place for you and Ellie to be right now. You need guidance I can't give you."

Parker looked over her shoulder. Ellie and Mabel and George were all staring at her. Ellie looked like she was about to cry.

"How long?" she whispered.

"Just the eight weeks we discussed," her father reassured her.

"What happens after that?" Parker asked. "We come home and pretend this never happened?"

"Well, no," he replied. "There are options. You do have certain responsibilities. Mabel and George will help you and your sister understand what that looks like, and I'll be there to support you both."

"OK," Parker said. She felt small and scared and uncomfortable with everyone listening. "I love you, Dad."

"I love you too, sweetheart. Be brave. I'm so proud of you, Parker."

Parker passed the phone to Ellie. While Ellie regaled their dad with tales about Arlo, Parker watched the flames dance in the fireplace and considered the situation. Something was happening that someone wasn't saying; that was clear.

And Parker was going to find out what it was.

"Are there any books around here?" Parker asked as Ellie wrapped up the call and joined them by the fire. Someone had told Parker once that you could learn everything you needed to know about a person from their bookshelf. So if she was going to get answers about Mabel and George and Haven, she may as well start there.

"Of course," Mabel told her. "Just go up the spiral stairs off the kitchen and take a left through the air duct tunnel. You might have to crawl, but if I can fit through, you definitely can. Then you'll see three miniature doorways. They were made for children's playhouses, I think. Anyway, pick the midsize one of the three and you'll find yourself in our library. There are all kinds of books there."

Parker stared at her blankly.

"We also have some things near the fireplace. You're welcome to help yourself." Mabel moved toward a shelf in the corner of the room that was jam-packed with what Parker at first joyfully assumed were magazines. She hefted a stack to the floor next to Parker. Parker picked up a copy and noted the matching gray covers on each book.

"What are these?"

"Issues of the *Farmers' Almanac*," Mabel replied, returning to her seat in front of the fire. "Exciting stuff! You're welcome."

A quick look told Parker everything she needed to know about an almanac, which turned out to be a book about dirt and the weather. Parker managed to read two full pages before abandoning them to Ellie, who seemed to find them fascinating.

"It's mostly about rain," Parker grumbled.

Ellie's eyes widened. "Cool!"

"All yours."

"There's one of these for every year!" Ellie cheered, paging through 1967's almanac, clearly pleased. "Awesome. Just think, we can track weather patterns over the decades to see if there's anything cyclical happening."

"Great." Parker fought back an eyeroll.

George and Mabel looked at Ellie fondly as she paged through nature articles, and Parker proceeded to stare at the fire some more. Mabel and George soon dozed off, and Parker watched the embers pulse with a dying red glow, lulled by the sound of her relatives snoring in a strange, soothing harmony. It wasn't very late at night—probably no later than eight—but Parker supposed when you were as ancient as Mabel and

George and had mucked around on a farm all day, life was probably pretty tiring. Nevertheless, there were only so many minutes Parker could spend looking at a flame jumping over and around a piece of wood.

"I've got to go to the bathroom," Parker eventually told Ellie. It wasn't true, but it seemed nicer than *I will scream at the top of my lungs if I have to sit here doing nothing for one more second.*

"Don't forget to flush with the rainwater," Ellie replied, not bothering to look up from her article about weeds.

Ugh. Ellie was nauseatingly responsible sometimes.

Parker headed upstairs to her bedroom and grabbed her journal and a pen from the nightstand. Maybe she would write until she fell asleep. But of course no part of her was sleepy; she'd slept so late that morning, she felt like she might never sleep again.

She thought back to what Mabel had said about a library. At first, Parker had thought her aunt was pulling her leg. But it was true that she hadn't seen much of the house, despite Mabel and George having promised a tour with "all the bells and whistles."

Probably literal bells and whistles, Parker realized. Recycled bells and whistles and a drum set or three.

Was there an actual library hidden behind a Goldilocks-style, midsize door? If so, what else could Haven House be hiding? Parker peeked out of her bedroom and examined the corridor. If Ellie's bedroom door was concealed behind a bookcase, there were probably other secret things. She tucked her journal and pen in her overalls' bib pocket—the nice thing about overalls was that they had a million pockets—and moved slowly down the hallway, pressing every panel and opening every built-in cupboard, feeling for secret hideaways. Nothing exciting except for a giant stash of Q-tips, which Parker was grateful for but also found suspicious.

Then she remembered to look up.

Bingo.

Sure enough, there was a hatch in the ceiling. If Parker stood on the built-in shelving opposite Ellie's bedroom door, she could just reach the hatch. She hooked her index finger in the little metal pull and yanked it down.

Parker dropped back from the shelf to the floor, pulling the hidden staircase with her.

Every house had its own smell. Once, before Parker knew Clara had started having a bunch of fun without her, she and Clara had discussed this fact and they'd decided that you were immune to your own house smell. For instance, Clara didn't know her house smelled like a mall candle store, just like Parker didn't know her house smelled like something burnt to a crisp in the oven until Clara told her so. Once you lived in a place long enough, its smell disappeared. Or else you went *noseblind* to it—a term she'd learned from a laundry detergent commercial featuring smelly gym socks that gave off green cartoon stink lines.

Now standing alone at the top of a concealed staircase made of wine corks and deflated basketballs, Parker took a big whiff of Haven House, which was extra pungent up high. (Did odors rise the same way hot air did?) Perhaps snooping was wrong. Perhaps Parker was taking advantage of her older relatives' obvious inexperience with the ways of kids. Everyone had pretty much left her alone since the incident in the woods, and Parker considered this a win, since she had been breaking the rules by going into the woods in the first place. Should she really break the rules further by snooping without permission?

The clear answer was yes.

After all, no one had said anything about *not* snooping. Mabel had encouraged Parker to crawl through an air duct less than an hour ago. There was a lot of snooping to do in Haven House, Parker was realizing, and a lot of stairs made out of weird things. But in every part of the house she'd been in so far, there was only one smell: a distinct odor she couldn't quite place.

"Campfire," she said out loud, as if hearing her voice could pin it down, fasten something elusive to her sense of reality.

Standing alone at the top of a staircase saying a word like *campfire* was an alarmingly Ellie-like thing to do, but whatever. At least she wasn't carrying around a fish in a bag and muttering things to a dog when she thought no one noticed.

"Fettuccini alfredo," she said, chasing the house smell as it seemed to morph into a totally different scent—rich and savory, there and gone. Frustrated, she leaned forward a bit and sniffed again.

"Lavender soap?" She shook her head. "Whatever, Haven. I give up."

A stray thought, nearly as tough to pin down as the smell, came and went. Everything in Haven House was connected in this ramshackle, ever-shifting way—the walls and doors made of odds and ends (or *bits and bobs,* as she'd overheard George saying), the floor plan that seemed to be some kind of architectural prank, the spiraling corridors to nowhere in particular.

Parker turned her back on the staircase and headed down a hallway lined with papier-mâché paneling. Glimpses of old-timey newspaper ads speckled the walls—names of products that sounded like fantasy creatures, Borax, Renuzit, Fels-Naptha. Things with multiple-striped limbs and British accents. She trailed a finger across the smooth, shiny panels. Had her mother's fingertips brushed against the same lacquered ads? Had she *made* them herself? Had she been a kid

Parker might have liked before she turned into a grown-up who abandoned her family on a whim?

The retro newspapers gave way to a series of alcoves. Each dim recess set deep into the wall contained patchwork footwear displayed like museum pieces on small pedestals: boots sewn from denim (the same soft, pale blue material that her Haven overalls were made of), sandals fashioned out of twine and rubber bands.

"Where *am* I?" Parker said out loud.

As if in answer, rain began to drum on the roof of Haven House. It sounded like it was coming from just above her head and off to the side, beyond the alcoves. Parker stopped in her tracks. Unless she was completely turned around, she was on the third of four floors—up two sets of stairs from the living room, where George and Mabel's whistling snores had ribboned up into the rafters. So she must be on one of those creepy jutting out layers, the ones that seemed to float in midair like Tetris pieces, widening the house at the top so it looked upside-down. Parker hopped in place a few times, half expecting the house to collapse beneath her. How *did* this structure work?

As she was puzzling it out, Ellie popped out of one of the alcoves, Arlo padding at her heels, causing Parker to shriek.

"Try knocking next time!" she said, somewhat nonsensically. "Where did you come from?"

Ellie looked pretty flummoxed herself. She turned around in a full circle, then stared at Parker, blinking. "I have no idea," she said. "I wish we'd gotten the whole house tour yesterday to prevent getting lost like this today. Do *you* know where we are?"

"Nope," Parker said. "George and Mabel obviously aren't used to having kids around. I think we can chalk up the tour oversight to tragedy. Betrayal. Forces beyond our control. Just like every single other thing that's happened since we turned twelve."

Ellie was silent for a moment. Then she looked downward. "No, *you* are," she said, presumably to Arlo. Ellie shook her head ruefully. "There's a sick cow," she explained to Parker. "I needed to get my mind off it so . . . we were just sort of looking at the back of this rusty old car, have you seen that? Like, there's part of a car *in* the house, and honestly it doesn't seem super safe, and then there was this passageway *through* the car, and then we were here."

"What does this place smell like to you?" Parker asked. It was the longest non-argument conversation she'd had with her sister in a while, she realized.

Ellie scrunched up her face and sniffed the air. "Peppermint tea," she said. Then she was silent for a moment. Then she paused. "You're right, that's closer," she said to Arlo. The dog nipped gently at her leg, then stretched his long forepaws out in front of him, claws clacking on the scuffed, knotted hardwood floor.

"Care to share?" Parker said wryly.

"Oh. Arlo says spearmint gum. His nose is a lot keener than ours."

"Ellie..." Parker started. She was starting to worry that Ellie's fantasies were getting out of hand.

"I know what you're going to say," Ellie's eyes flickered to Arlo, who yawned. "But I'm not crazy. You know how different things are here. I've been wanting to talk to you about it."

"Tell him not to eat my toothbrush again."

"Remember what George said when we first got here? We close ourselves off to the unexpected. We dismiss things we don't understand."

Parker shifted uncomfortably. All day long, she'd been trying to forget the things that had happened in the woods that she didn't understand. She gestured around at the alcoves with their footwear exhibits. "I would love to understand all this, believe me," she said wryly. She pointed at the ceiling, which was made of tin embossed with oblong shapes. "And can you hear *that*?"

Ellie paused, frowning. "Rain on the roof."

"Right. On the third-floor protrusion. I'd sure like to know how this entire house manages to defy gravity. It's like we're floating."

Ellie shrugged. "Your guess is as good as mine. Parker, about the woods—"

Arlo grew animated, jumping up and placing his fore-paws against Ellie's overalls. His tongue flopped eagerly from his open mouth.

"Does he have to pee?" Parker asked.

Ellie paused for a moment, as if listening. "No," she said. "But they do." She pointed down the corridor, a dim blotch of space that stretched toward some hazy ending, a dead end or sharp turn, near or far, impossible to tell.

A pair of roosters strutted out of the shadows. Ellie laughed at something Parker couldn't hear. The roosters paid them no mind as they passed. "They must have come in through one of the doggie slots in the door-walls," Ellie told her.

Roosters seem like jerks, Parker thought. The kind of bird that sits at the cool-kids' table, away from the lesser poultry.

Arlo barked once, met Ellie's eyes, and headed for the last alcove on the left.

"Come on," Ellie tugged on the strap of Parker's overalls.

"Um, yeah. Let's follow Arlo into a dark hole," Parker said. "Great idea." But she had to admit, she was curious. And didn't dogs have good survival instincts? Sure.

Arlo disappeared into the alcove. Ellie and Parker fol-lowed. For a moment, they were lost in a pitch-black tunnel. The rain was suddenly very loud, hammering an unseen roof.

And there was a hollow sound to it too, like they were stepping into a—

Giant glass globe.

It was like entering the heart of the storm, except they weren't getting wet. The deluge pounded the glass dome above their heads, and beyond it the night sky loomed. Even in the nearly full darkness, Parker could sense the low, thick, roiling clouds, which were like a sodden gray blanket tossed into the heavens.

Thunder split the night.

Parker's hands tingled. She felt a sharp jolt of *something* like what she'd felt in the woods.

Arlo wagged his tail, ecstatic and jumpy.

"A solarium," Ellie said. "I read about these in one of the almanacs."

"It must be *between* the rooms on this floor," Parker said. "Because we definitely can't see this from out front. Like, there's an empty space in the middle of the house, open to the sky."

"It's so dark," Ellie said.

"Yeah," Parker said absently. Her hands tingled once again, cued by her sister's words. She twisted them together. No. What happened in the woods would not happen again. A thought formed in the recesses of her mind—something she'd halfway observed and filed away without really noticing exactly. *It's so dark.*

"There are no light switches," Parker mentioned.

"What?"

"Anywhere in the house. No light switches. Think about it—Mabel and George are the kind of people who *flush toilets with trough water*. Their guilty pleasure is a stash of Q-tips. There's no Wi-Fi. Doesn't even seem to be any electricity, other than that ancient phone. So what's been lighting up the kitchen, the bedrooms, and the hallways last night and today? Why is there light whenever we need it, and none when we don't?"

"Um," Ellie said. "There's some kind of lantern over here."

Parker peered into the gloom. Her sister was right: A glass cylinder dangled from a hook embedded in one of the wooden beams that supported the glass dome. Ellie poked at it.

"There's no switch."

A sudden flash, a bright jagged seam in the night sky. Parker blinked into the afterglow. Imprinted upon her vision was a glimpse of the solarium's interior. Lush greenery, impossibly thick tendrils, ferns the size of dinner plates . . .

Parker's hands felt different. Tingly, yes, but *alive*. Similar to the way they'd felt in the woods, but without the fear and anxiety. As if some ecstatic new force was twitching just beneath her skin, hummingbird-quick, and it was hers to control instead of some wild thing that made her bad or scary or freakish. She recognized the same heady exhilaration she'd always felt on a field or a court. Like it was up to her to determine what happened next.

Her hands felt—what was the word?—*receptive* to the lightning. Like they'd just received a message and were busy composing a lively reply.

"Ellie . . . yesterday in the woods . . ."

Ellie stopped, giving her a look. "Yes? They told us not to go back there. Parker, what happened to you there?"

"Nothing," Parker said quickly. "I just . . . I got scared, and I felt weird, and I'm feeling sort of like that now—"

"Weird how? Weird *sick*?"

"No, weird like—"

Her hands exploded before she could finish her thought. Parker cried out as time slowed to reveal exactly what was happening to her in exacting detail. The skin on her palms was briefly translucent, exposing what had just been jumping underneath—a landscape of sparks, a million bright pinpricks, all of them screaming and clawing to get *out out out* into the world—

Time snapped back into place. Acrid smoke curled up from her hands. Gasping for breath, Parker held them in front of her face.

She was completely unscathed.

She felt no pain.

"Um," Ellie said. "Parker?"

Parker lowered her hands. Her sister was standing there, shell-shocked. Next to her, the lantern burned as bright as the North Star. The whole solarium was illuminated. Parker had lit it up.

Above, the rain slowed to a weak patter.

Ellie's eyes were wide. "Maybe now's the time to officially convey that I can talk to animals. Like, really talk to them. As in, not just Arlo. And I'm not pretending. I can really hear their thoughts." She offered Parker a weak smile.

"Right. So . . . I think we have a lot to catch up on." Parker took a deep breath. "But not right this second. I'm feeling a little dizzy. Think you can ask Arlo here to navigate us back to our bedrooms? How is this house so confusing? You can *talk* talk to animals?" It was kind of a lot to process. Ellie nodded. Then Parker noticed Ellie staring at her hands.

"Oh god! I swear I won't hurt you," Parker said. "Please don't be afraid of me, Ellie."

"It's not that," Ellie told her. "I only just noticed . . . you're wearing your bracelet from Mom."

Parker opened her mouth to make an excuse, but before she could say a word, Ellie wrapped her in a giant hug. "I think we've found each other again," she whispered.

Parker melted into her. Truthfully, she felt the same. But she also felt something else deep inside, something she couldn't acknowledge to Ellie. It was the same something that she'd felt in the woods—an unknowable part of her she couldn't escape. Fear of what she could have done if she *had* lost control. A danger.

CHAPTER TWELVE

The girls had been at Haven for less than a week, but it was already strange to think that there had ever been a life outside the sanctuary. Ellie's eyes opened the next morning before Mabel even called them to breakfast. It was like she could feel the world shifting into morning outside her window, as if the sun made a sound as it pulled itself out of the ground and into the sky.

"I know that's not what actually happens," Ellie told Walter.

Pretty sure the earth is swimming around the sun out in space, Walter said.

"Right," Ellie nodded, pulling on her socks, and wondered just how Walter knew about space.

Breakfast, Ellie thought, taking in the spread Aunt Mabel and George had arranged with great care across the rough-hewn logs of the dining room table. Felix had come early to take Toffee to the emergency vet, only to discover

Toffee had begun to improve in the night. It was decided that Toffee would stay put for now, with close monitoring.

"Thank goodness," George had said, holding a hand to his heart. "That's a very good sign." With him, Felix had brought a veritable feast.

"Won't you join us?" Mabel asked.

"Can't stay," Felix had replied. "Going to check on the rest of the animals and head home to help my dad set up shop at the farmers market downtown."

Now Ellie, Parker, and Mabel and George were enjoying the spoils of Ray's baking: a plate of steaming scones with freshly churned and whipped butter, alongside slices of apple and pear tart. How different from the Pop-Tarts she and Parker often gobbled down cold in the car on the way to school in Harborville.

Ellie tried to focus on the food, to let herself enjoy it. She thought back to the rhubarb patch she'd helped George water and till the day before and wondered if the plant would take to the soil. The sheer effort the task had involved made her appreciate the simple wonder of the meal in front of her. It seemed important to stay connected. But she was too distracted to enter the kind of state her Aunt Mabel and George seemed to occupy all the time: attuned to the land, appreciative of its gifts yet respectful of its autonomy.

This morning, though, there wasn't any time for daydreaming. George cleared his throat. It was so delicate a sound, it may as well have been made by a hummingbird. Still, Parker and Ellie each paused midbite. George didn't need to be loud to command a room.

"We have some things we need to discuss," George told them.

Ellie's heart accelerated. It was hard to believe they'd only been there three days and they were about to directly address things Ellie wouldn't have dared say aloud in ordinary circumstances. And Mabel and George didn't even know what had happened in the solarium. When Ellie closed her eyes, she could still see the bright, jagged flashes that seemed to jump eagerly from her sister's hands, quick as—well . . .

Quick as lightning.

Ellie swallowed hard. There was a long, uncomfortable silence.

Breakfast! Arlo said from underneath the table, making Ellie jump. He was clearly impatient for the people-food scraps he technically wasn't allowed to eat but had been regularly receiving via Ellie's secretive hands.

Why isn't anyone saying anything? Ellie was suddenly hyperaware of the weight of the box in her lap, which she'd pulled from underneath the floorboards in her room, and the even weightier sense of what she'd discovered inside . . .

"Ray Findlay made this rhubarb jam fresh this morning," George said in an offhand way, offering a small brass urn full of crimson goo. The urn was etched with the lion and earth symbols the girls had on their overalls. "Have you two seen the patch today?" He nodded toward the window over her shoulder. "Bit of a surplus." He winked.

Ellie glanced out the window and felt her jaw drop. The rhubarb patch, yesterday a small square of tilled earth where a few anemic stalks sprouted, had become as lush and over-grown as the strange plants in the solarium. Huge floppy green leaves swayed lazily atop thick red tubers. The rhubarb plants seemed to be fighting for space, crowding the little patch, already creeping out into the yard surrounding it.

Next to Ellie, Parker squirmed a little in her seat, vibrat-ing nervous energy. Ellie clutched the box in her lap a little harder. What was George getting at?

"Breakfast is the second-most important meal of the day," Mabel added. "You girls should eat up!"

Even Parker couldn't resist taking the bait. "I thought it was *the* most important meal of the day."

Common misconception! Arlo said.

"That's what you've been taught, is it?" George said slyly.

"OK, OK," Parker said, and Ellie braced herself for the rapid-fire tumble of words that always came out whenever her sister's pent-up nerves unspooled. "Before you tell us something like *the most important meal of the day is what you feed your head* or some other weird hippie thing that's supposed to be a lesson but doesn't make any sense, can we please just be direct and get to the point for once?" she trailed off to catch her breath. "You said we needed to talk. So let's talk! And not in code!" Normally Ellie wouldn't have appreciated her sister's rudeness, but in this case she agreed. George and Mabel were not the best communicators at times.

Here we go, Arlo said. She heard him sigh as he curled up under the table and rested his head on his forepaws.

"We were treading gently," George explained. "After all, Parker, you were a bit sensitive yesterday."

"But I, for one, am glad you're so receptive today," Mabel added. "Let's cut to the chase, then. George tells me Ellie can communicate with animals." Ellie had been bracing herself for this exact conversation, but Mabel didn't seem the least bit perturbed.

"That's right." Ellie nodded. "Not all animals, though. Just Toffee the cow and my fish, Walter. Oh, and Arlo, of course."

Leave me out of this, if you don't mind, Arlo said.

"Not all animals *so far,*" George corrected.

"Well. I suppose so." It hadn't occurred to Ellie that there might be more to her new ability. She wondered briefly what any normal person would do if she told them she could talk to animals. Probably laugh in her face.

"Hmm." George steepled his fingers. Mabel pursed her lips.

Then they turned to look at Parker.

For once, Ellie's sister seemed tongue-tied. She held up her hands.

"Lightning," she said. "Kind of."

Mabel turned to George and raised an eyebrow. "That's a new one," she said.

George nodded. "Interesting." He began buttering a scone. "I wouldn't have pegged you for that skill, Parker, at least not right away."

"Girls," Mabel began. "We admit, we wanted you to have time to grow more comfortable in your new surroundings before you fully realized your powers but if I can be completely honest, this rather accelerated timeline is for the best."

Ellie locked eyes with her sister. *Powers?!* Mabel had said this so matter-of-factly, it felt like Ellie was dreaming.

Powers. Of course. No big deal. Shrug.

"You *knew* this would happen?" Parker said.

"Of course," George said. "It's why we brought you to Haven in the first place."

Ellie swallowed hard. "Does Dad know?"

"Yes," Mabel said. "He observed a few things that made him think your powers were beginning to emerge, even before the onset of your twelfth birthday."

"I didn't ask to come here," Parker frowned. "I was happy where I was."

"I know you don't like it here," Mabel began. "I know you think it's hard. It *is* hard. Your father sent you here be—"

"Our father lied to us," Parker interrupted.

"Because," Mabel pressed forward, "he saw what was happening to you."

Parker squeezed her fists by her sides. She could feel her fingers digging into her palms like red-hot pokers.

"At the basketball court," Mabel clarified. "Your father saw you."

Parker closed her eyes. The night of their birthday. On the basketball court. The crack in the ground beneath her feet.

"It w-was an earthquake," she stammered.

"Sometimes," Mabel said, tugging her sleeve, "we are earthquakes." There on Mabel's wrist was a silver bracelet. Just like Ellie's and like Parker's. "Your dad didn't want to spend the summer without you," Mabel continued. "But he knew it was necessary for your development. It's different for everyone, but the powers typically manifest when you mature."

"So for me and Ellie, you mean when we get our periods," Parker clarified. Ellie looked at Parker. Had she gotten her period? Ellie hadn't. How did Ellie not know Parker had gotten her period? They were twins! Didn't twins do everything the same?

"Well, no," Mabel said. "That's a very literal interpretation. But they do tend to pop up around the same time. You're at that age when you're changing physically and emotionally. Those changes trigger latent powers in people who have them."

"But why do we have them in the first place?" Parker looked put upon. "I just want to be a normal kid and go to school and play basketball with my friends. Why did we have to come to Haven? What is the point of all of this?" Frustrated, she let her fork clatter to the table.

Ellie wondered if Parker had told Clara about her period.

"You inherited your gifts from your mother," Mabel explained patiently. "They run in our side of the family. Haven is where your mother came when her powers first emerged, to hone them and discover the bounds of her capabilities. She wanted you to come here too, when it was time."

"Um," Ellie said, lifting the box from her lap and dropping it on the table with dramatic flair. *Plunk.* "Did you know about *this* too?"

She opened the box. Her sister reached in and took out a handful of photos. Ellie took the rest. Together, they fanned the prints out on the table. Parker's hand found Ellie's. There was Ginny, their mother, when she was their age, lacing up her roller skates on the path that skirted the edge of Haven's pond. There she was, a little older, milking a spotted cow in the fields by the stone wall. And there she was, older still, wearing a flowy dress on a late summer afternoon, reading underneath a stately old oak tree.

"Oh yes," murmured Mabel. "Where did you find these?"

"Under the floor in my room," Ellie replied.

George laughed. "That's so like Ginny." He tapped a fingertip gently against a photo of their mother cooking something in a cast-iron pot over a campfire. "I took this one."

"Her famous root vegetable stew," Mabel said, laughing until tears came to her eyes. "It was very . . . earthy."

"Cooking was certainly *not* one of her 'gifts,'" George chuckled.

"This was also in the box," Ellie said, placing the note from Sadie on the table.

"Ah," George said. He and Mabel exchanged a look.

"So? Who is she?"

There was a long pause.

"Ginny and Sadie were best friends," Mabel finally said.

"No," Parker said, her eyes narrowed. "That can't be true."

George looked startled. "What do you mean?"

"Mom never mentioned anyone named Sadie. If they were such good friends, we would have known. Unless Mom just had this whole secret life she never told us about. Oh wait, yeah, that tracks."

"Do *not* speak that way of your mother," George said, his

voice sharp. Parker leaned back in her chair, stunned. George had never spoken that way to them.

"You girls are who you are because of Ginny," Mabel said sternly. She tapped the picture of their mother lacing up her skates. "Her legacy. She was a wonder."

"Sorry," Parker mumbled, looking abashed.

Ellie eyed the girl in the photos. So according to Mabel, there was a direct line between the smiling, happy kid in silver sparkly skates with her whole life ahead of her, and Ellie's newfound ability to talk to animals.

OK.

Next to her, Parker looked down at her hands.

"We know it's a lot to take in," Mabel said, resting a hand on George's arm. "Believe it or not, we had this exact same conversation with your mom when she was your age. She didn't take it well either when her dad brought her here. Her mom married into this family and she never even knew about Ginny's abilities. Think how hard that would have been. You two share this with your mom. It's a gift she left you. It's something special."

"How does it all . . . work?" Ellie asked shyly.

"I'll do my best to explain." George took a breath, seeming calmer now. "We hold this thing in our hands," he said. "This power. It is ours and has been for as long as anyone can remember. It is ours to carry."

"It's bigger than us," Mabel added.

"If we aren't careful with it, the balance can tip," George continued. "Our relationship to the planet is unique. We can't fix everything, even though it's tempting to try. Interfering with natural cycles can be dangerous. Think about where we live. Sometimes wildfires clear brush, and that's good. It's when circumstances tip too far in one direction and balance is lost—when wildfires rage out of control, for example—that things go bad."

"It really is just about understanding there are two sides to a coin," Mabel said. "The trouble is that people tend to take from our planet without giving back. That's where we come in—to fix the problems caused by greed."

"You can see it in every change in weather patterns; every oil slick that chokes the life out of the oceans; every ancient forest clear-cut to make way for the endless sprawl of our cities."

Mabel nodded in agreement and leaned forward. "It's up to us to reset the balance so our planet doesn't go totally out of whack. But it's hard when other people don't respect the earth. That's when the Danger comes in. The Danger is a malevolent, shape-shifting force created by people's greed. It is a monster that feeds off human error. It gets bigger and more formidable every time anyone takes away from our planet without giving back. It wants to destroy those of us with powers, because it knows we're its enemy. And it has a nose for weakness. It finds people who it thinks will easily stray and consumes them. The Darkness will win when it has rid our planet of its protectors."

"Oh, yes. Anytime chemicals are expelled from factories into bodies of water, murdering marine life, you'd better believe the Danger is getting stronger. Through it all, Haven House has remained just that," George said. "A haven from the Danger. A place of rest, reconnection, and learning. Our worry now is that the Danger will get strong enough to destroy Haven. We've managed to keep it at bay, but it's always after us. Because if it destroys those of us with powers . . . well. Then there'll be nothing to stand in its way, and our beloved planet will be kaput."

"It's an actual monster?" Parker wanted to know.

"Indeed. But here, you're safe," George assured them. "At least for the time being. Inside the stone walls of the grounds of Haven, the Danger cannot pass. Now that you know the truth, you can help us restore harmony. In simple terms, our powers support environmental activism."

"You can use your power alone, but it works best if you work together with someone, all the better if you've got a sibling counterpart. Two is the magic number! The two of you"—Mabel pointed to Ellie and Parker—"balance each other out. And that helps with overall balance. When you are at odds with your sister, the Danger can sense it."

"That's why Mabel and I still live together," George said

sweetly. "It's not as if single life chose us. I had dozens of suitors. One of them was royalty. But here I am, playing house with my sister forty years later." He took a bite of tart.

Mabel scoffed. "Ingvar was low-ranking royalty in one of those countries you can rent out by the week. Good thing Ray's around now." She gave George a sly grin, which George pretended not to notice.

Ellie and Parker exchanged amused glances.

Got that? Arlo said to Ellie from underneath the table.

"Um," Ellie said.

"I'm not living with Ellie for the rest of my life," Parker informed them.

"I'm not living with *you* for the rest of *my* life," Ellie shot back, hurt.

"You'll probably live in a barn with all your animals," Parker said, as if that were an insult.

Outside, a clap of thunder sounded.

"Well!" Mabel straightened. "That's certainly enough classified earth-magic information for one country breakfast. And enough bickering." Ellie had the feeling there was something Mabel wasn't telling them.

"Eat, eat," George said. "You've hardly touched your food. We thought we might deliver some bushels of rhubarb to the farmers market before the storm kicks in. We have way too much for all the rhubarb tarts in the world."

Head spinning, Ellie glanced out the window.

It had been a perfectly sunny day when they sat down to breakfast. Clear blue sky stretching into infinity.

"The weather here is very strange," she commented. "When I woke up, I never would have thought there was a storm coming."

Mabel dragged a knife through the bowl of butter and slapped a dollop onto a still-warm scone. "Oh, child. Lately, there is always a storm coming."

After breakfast, Parker went outside with Mabel and George to help cultivate the abundance of rhubarb. Ellie muttered something about needing to put away the box of photographs and excused herself from the chore. Mabel and George didn't press the issue—and surprisingly, neither did Parker, though Ellie couldn't escape her sister's raised-eyebrow inquisition, as everyone knew Ellie would normally be first at any garden task.

Back in her bedroom, she pocketed Sadie's note for later and had just tucked the photograph box into a nightstand made from a bisected tuba when Arlo hopped onto her bed.

I know where you can find out more about everything George and Mabel were trying to tell you at breakfast.

Ellie folded her arms. "Honestly, that would be great. With

those two, it's like, the more they talk, the less I understand. It's very confusing about the Danger."

Arlo hesitated. *You got any treats?*

"No, why? Are you hungry?"

It's customary. When a dog does something good, or helpful, or impressive, or obedient, a human gives him a treat.

"Well, I'm not prepared at the moment. Do you like fish flakes?"

Arlo barked once in sheer disgust. *Never mind. Follow me.*

Ellie followed Arlo out into the hall, past several doors that served as walls. Doors with silver mail slots, doors with golden latches, doors with frosted-glass windows that looked out upon more doors. It was really very confusing not knowing which doors functioned as doors. Theoretically the house could extend endlessly, Ellie realized, or not at all. A chandelier cast nonelectric light through garlands of crystal prisms, speckling the wooden floor with tiny rainbows.

This way, this way.

Arlo took a sharp right turn through a brick archway from which strands of beads dangled and emerged into a windowless octagonal room. Each side of the octagon was a floor-to-ceiling bookcase. Each shelf was crammed with old volumes. Dust thickened the air. Ellie sneezed.

Gesundheit, Arlo said. *Anyway, it's all here. Books on advanced botany and earth history and intergenus communication.*

And much more. He stretched out on a hideous shag quilt and sighed dramatically. *Your treat deficit grows by the minute.*

Ellie scanned the nearest books' canvas-bound spines. "*The Language of Swallows: Grammar, Conjugation, Usage,*" she read aloud. "Wow."

That one's a total snooze, Arlo informed her.

"*Twinship Kinship: A Primer.*" Ellie kept reading. "*Berries: Friend or Foe?*"

She moved slowly around the room, absorbing titles that covered everything from owl poop to unseasonal humidity to armadillo incantations, tucking a few that interested her under her arm for later. Then she came to a rolltop desk made from petrified driftwood, upon which sat a book that caught her eye.

Etched into the cover of the book, in bright gold embossing, was an astrolabe—exactly like the one her mother had left behind for her and Parker. *How to Navigate the Cosmos in Six Easy Steps,* read the title.

"Funny that 'six easy steps' amounts to about five hundred pages," Ellie remarked to Arlo.

I've read it thrice, Arlo told her.

"You have not."

Arlo cocked his head as if to say, *Haven't I?*

Next to the cosmos book was a second book, much smaller, with a green, waxy cover. Ellie narrowed her eyes. Parker's journal! Somehow, her sister had been in this room before her. What had she been doing? After opening up about their powers and sharing in the discovery of their mom's photographs, Ellie had thought there weren't any secrets between them. It had felt like Ellie & Parker again, a unit, them versus the world, just like before Mom died.

Apparently, they were still keeping some things from each other.

Surprised by the heat that crept into her face and behind her ears, Ellie reached for the slender journal. She hesitated. She had never snooped in Parker's journal before. But how else could she find out what her sister had been doing in this strange library?

You could try asking her about it, Arlo volunteered. *Communication is sort of like transportation. The quickest way there is usually a straight line.*

"But then she could lie," Ellie reasoned, which she supposed was unfair, but this was too high stakes to risk it.

Humans. Arlo shook his head like he was shaking off rainwater. *So unnecessarily complicated.*

In the end, Ellie decided she would flip to a random entry. If that page didn't contain a clue to what Parker had been doing up here, then so be it—she wouldn't look any further. She wasn't about to spy on her sister's whole private life.

She took a deep breath and flipped to the last page. It was covered with Parker's chicken-scratch scrawl.

On it was a list of coordinates. Seemingly random numbers strung together and stacked atop one another in a pattern that somehow looked . . . familiar. Ellie peered closely at the list. Parker had written the names of places next to some of the coordinates, along with dates.

November 2, 1993, read one such entry. *Baton Rouge.* What could this possibly mean to Parker?

February 14, 2015. Permian Basin.

Ellie remembered that day. It was Valentine's Day, and their mom had been working on an oil spill in west Texas. She had called to tell them to look inside their suitcases for a special surprise. They'd each opened their suitcases to find them overflowing with heart-shaped chocolates and dozens of paper cutout hearts on which she'd written the things she loved about Ellie and Parker. It had been the last Valentine's Day their mom had been alive. It was stuff like that that made Ellie know their mom really had died. She would never have abandoned them.

Ellie's eyes traveled down the list, pausing each time Parker had written a location next to the coordinates. Some of the places she recognized, some she didn't. Ellie wrinkled her brow, trying to picture the lower Kennebec on a map.

Then it hit her. *A map.* These coordinates looked exactly like the ones Parker had pointed out next to the world map hanging on the wall of Ellie's bedroom. Parker had been snooping too, then. And she had somehow figured out how to use the astrolabe, a gift their mom had given *both* of them, which Ellie had stowed away in the bedroom nightstand.

With the righteousness particular to someone who's been betrayed, Ellie flipped to the next page. This one was filled with paragraphs. She pored over Parker's messy writing. *Oh, Parker,* Ellie thought. She flipped to another page, guilt setting in. And another, scanning quickly.

This wasn't a journal at all, at least not in the regular way. It was an investigative notebook, like in that book *Harriet the Spy* they'd loved so much as kids. Every single page contained a theory about their mom's disappearance, and none of them was the theory Parker had always claimed to believe—that their mom had purposefully abandoned them. Instead, the pages were filled with notions of underground lairs and UFOs.

Ellie glanced back at the list of coordinates and shook her head, feeling sad. Whatever this was, Parker hadn't told Ellie because it wasn't real. It was another rejection of reality; another bubble Ellie might burst. Because each theory Parker came up with had one thing in common: hope. As long as their mother was trapped in a submarine in the Bermuda Triangle, she might still come back.

Parker was angry, all right. But she wasn't angry at their mom, Ellie realized now. She was angry at the world that had taken her away.

CHAPTER THIRTEEN

"I'm not sure who will want all this rhubarb," Parker said doubtfully. She hauled another load into the back of the truck, her arms aching. The clouds overhead looked ominous. Every time she returned for a new load, it seemed the rhubarb they'd harvested had grown back, and then some.

"You'd be surprised by how excited people get about freebies," George told her. "People will take anything that's free. Even free manure for compost! But we never charge for anything Haven produces."

All around them, Parker realized, Haven seemed to be springing to life. Sprouts were emerging from the soil with cute little minty green curls. The cow Ellie treated like a pet was standing up and limping around and *moo*ing all the time.

Although maybe to Ellie the mooing was more than just a moo?

The chickens, according to George, were also doing well and plumping right up, although it was pretty clear they didn't like Parker. Even when she'd scattered seed in front of their coop, they acted like she was a waiter or something. "You're rude, OK?" Parker had snapped at the rooster that glared at her with its little yellow eyes as she tossed the last of the feed. Parker would have to ask Ellie whether her suspicions were correct, and the poultry was saying impolite things about her.

As they hauled rhubarb, George and Mabel chattered on about the sheep and the grass and whether or not to expand the paddock for more ailing animals. Parker was already hot and sticky and tired. She wanted to be playing Ultimate alongside Clara. She wanted someone to talk about something other than the farm and their mom and their gifts. It could be anything! Books! Basketball? Politics? Music? The joy of sugar? Ancient philosophers? The world? She wanted to be anywhere else.

"Hey, Mabel, what's your favorite part of the world?" Parker tried, thinking of her mother's map on the wall.

Mabel gave her a funny look. "One place is just as good as any other," she said in a tone that implied Parker was daft. It wasn't like Parker was trying to rate the countries on a scale of one to ten or anything. She wasn't going to be *judgmental* about the left-out places. Jeez.

They harvested, hauled, and dumped until Parker was dripping with sweat. The weather vanes Ellie had plunked in the yard, she noticed, were going mental. They were spinning like crazy and stopping, spinning again, and stopping.

The lion one was pointed toward the forest, and the one with the earth symbol pointed toward the main road to town. It was strange since there wasn't any kind of breeze, but they'd always been broken. Parker stopped to drink from a jug full of filtered well water that Mabel had brought out. The air hung thick and damp around her. She swiped at her sweaty brow with her sweaty bare arm, which only made things worse.

She felt Mabel watching her and turned. Mabel's features seemed to soften. "You're a good little worker," she said. Then she handed Parker a fresh handkerchief out of the seemingly endless supply she kept in her bib pocket. "An underrated accessory," she joked. "Tell all your friends."

"I would if I could." Parker wasn't even trying to be smart. She was just sad.

"This was *going* to be a surprise," Mabel told her, tucking the last bushel of rhubarb into the bed of the truck, "but since you're looking a little down, maybe it'll cheer you up to know the library is just down the block from the farmers market."

"And the library has that Google you love so much," George remarked.

"INTERNET!" Parker shrieked, jumping up and down. Her spirits instantly lifted. She could swear even the sky brightened a little. She hugged George, nearly tackling him, then threw her arms around Mabel, who looked pleased (if slightly stunned). "Hurray, hurray, HURRAY!" Parker shouted.

She could talk to Clara, who'd probably been emailing her like crazy. She would get to hear about CUT orientation and about school and whether Ever Natoli had said yes or no to Iris Dimos when she asked her out in a note the day of Parker's birthday. And anything else she'd missed in the three long days since she'd left Harborville.

Five whole minutes later—which was the interminable length of time it had taken to track down Ellie, who'd been deep in conversation with her fish—they were piled into the front of the truck and easing down the drive.

"Take care of the house, Arlo!" Ellie shouted out the window. Parker gave her a look. "What? He likes having a task."

Rather than turning left toward the train station, they took a right and drove for ten minutes along winding country roads. Mabel hugged the sharp bends with ease, as though she'd had a past life driving getaway cars. "I've had to drive in many challenging places," she explained when Parker pointed it out. "When you've steered an RV from one end of Los Angeles to another, you've done it all."

"Why were you driving an RV through L.A.?" Ellie asked, looking interested for the first time since they'd begun the drive.

"Technically it was a pop up camper hitched to a truck," Mabel said, as if that cleared it up. After a moment she added,

"I went to offer help to some friends in need. Who wants ice cream later?" And that was that.

"Deer," said George and Ellie simultaneously. Mabel slowed.

"I don't see any—" Parker started. "Whoa." A deer bounded out of the forest into their path a few seconds later. "How did you spot that?" Parker asked her sister.

"I didn't," Ellie replied, looking unhappy. "I just knew."

"What's wrong?"

Ellie's face looked drawn, and her lips were pressed in a thin line. "Don't you feel it?" she asked.

"Feel what?" Parker was confused. All she felt was excitement at the prospect of finally connecting with her friends back home. Up front, Mabel and George were pretending to focus on the road, but Parker could tell they were listening.

"It's like a heavy weight is pressing on us, the farther we go from Haven," Ellie explained. "At least that's how it feels to me."

"You're just as safe in the world outside Haven as you ever were," Mabel said. "Safer now, maybe. You know of your gifts and you know of the Danger. You're armed with knowledge. This is just a regular trip to town, but it's also an opportunity for you to be in the world with what you know. That's the first step."

"To *what?*" Parker was a little mad. This thing—this *legacy*—had been foisted on them, and now they had no choice but to live with it. It wasn't fair. Now even a trip to town to use the Internet had A Bigger Meaning. So far, things at Haven were never simple. Why couldn't they be simple?

"Look," George said. "Just enjoy yourselves today. Bearsted is a lot of fun. I promise."

Overhead, there was a crack of thunder. Parker felt an insistent buzz in her palms. Come to think of it, the buzz had been there all day; it had begun to feel almost normal. But now the buzz moved to her heart. It was the same sort of feeling she got before a big game. Anticipation mixed with fear. Parker took a deep breath to center herself the way her coaches had taught her. She could let the buzzing overtake her, or she could be strong.

Parker chose strong. She always chose strong.

"I've always loved going into Bearsted," George said neutrally from the front. "Quite the adventure."

Parker glanced at Ellie again, and this time she registered fear in her sister's eyes. It had been a long time since they'd communicated in glances and nods, but Parker found that when she tried, she could still read her twin as easily as she could her own thoughts.

Danger, Ellie was communicating.

For the first time, Parker wondered if Mabel and George were telling them the whole truth.

"Why are we going to the farmers market if it's about to storm?" Parker asked, fighting to keep her voice even. She dug her fingernails into the old vinyl seat, trying to quiet her flaring palms. "You said we were safe inside Haven. What about in town?" Next to her, Ellie was staring out the window and twisting the whistle from Mom that she'd taken to wearing as a necklace.

George and Mabel exchanged a look. Parker recognized that look. It was the same thing she had just done with Ellie: a whole conversation in a glance. Parker felt the tingle spreading from her palms to her forearms.

"Tell us," she said. "Tell us now."

George half turned in his seat to face the girls. "Parker," he said in a soothing tone. "Please calm down. You're getting all worked up for nothing."

"I'm not," Parker said, as the heat began to travel to her face. "Why won't anyone say anything real?" Her palms were pulsing now, and she didn't dare look at them, instead shoving them beneath her thighs. "Why won't anyone just tell us the truth?"

"We aren't hiding anything from you," George protested. "You just need to trust us on this. There are things you aren't ready to hear."

"Why don't you try us?" Ellie asked.

"Not now." Mabel's voice filled the car. "You are the children, and we are the adults. That is how this works. We are in charge."

Now Parker was boiling mad. It simmered through her blood. It pulsed in her eardrums and her neck. She dared not move in case it spilled out of her, this anger, this *thing* that had taken on a life of its own.

"You're strangers," Ellie was saying next to her. Ellie's voice registered for Parker as if through a tunnel, muted behind the *thud thud thud* of her heart. "Why should we trust you? How do we know we can?" At that last note, Ellie's voice cracked, and Parker absorbed her fear. Ellie was afraid. Parker could not stand to see her sister afraid, and she would not allow people to push them around simply because they were grown-ups.

The surge of heat swept over her, and there was nothing more she could do to stop it. She closed her eyes and turned her palms face-up and even through her eyelids, she could see the light they cast. All the breath left her body, and there was only heat.

The world felt like it was on fire.

And it was all from her.

Parker opened her arms wide as the searing heat coursed through her and enveloped the palms of her hands.

She was overcome by a sense of total calm. She could see nothing, hear nothing, except for the tidal surge that carried her. Then there was a tremendous jolt. A sharp intake of breath. A small scream.

And for a while, all was still.

When Parker opened her eyes again, she and Ellie were alone in the truck and a mist had set in, obscuring her view. She blinked, waiting for her head to clear. Whatever had just happened was big, she knew—but she couldn't sort out exactly what. She could just make out Mabel and George, who were standing outside the vehicle, staring at something on the ground. Ellie was next to her, holding her hand. Her face looked pale and serious. Parker could feel Ellie's body trembling slightly.

"Are you OK?" Ellie asked.

"I don't know," Parker whispered. "What happened?"

"You got very hot, so hot I could feel it coming off you, and light came out of your hands," Ellie said. "And then . . . well. That happened." She pointed to the mountain side of the road. The rocky ledge was mostly uniform except for a gaping chunk in the middle, the space for the last missing piece of a puzzle.

Parker stared at her hand in Ellie's. Up until that moment, she'd thought it was a very-good-at-playing-frisbee-but-otherwise-regular hand. It still looked normal. Except a moment earlier, the force that had come from her had nearly killed them.

That day in the basketball court just before they'd left for Haven, she'd felt the asphalt crack under her feet. It wasn't like the earthquakes she'd felt before; it was as if something had traveled through her, broke through her, and cracked the ground.

She'd felt heat before too; all the time, really—she was always the sweatiest athlete. Clara even called her Hot Pants from the moment they'd first met. Her dad said she ran hot, and it was nothing to worry about. But it had never been like this, not even that night in the solarium with Ellie.

Parker removed her hand from Ellie's and opened the door, stepping onto the narrow country road. She could see now that the truck had swerved sideways, hard enough to leave skid marks on the pavement. To her right, there was the craggy edge of the mountain. To her left, massive trees formed a wall of green and rose endlessly into the mist like skyscrapers in a city.

"Parker!"

Parker squinted at Mabel and George. They stepped toward her, revealing the object they'd been examining.

The rock was large, the size of one of the truck's tires. It was nearly the height of Parker's knees. Parker began to shake. She recalled the weathervane with the earth symbol, which had been pulling frantically toward the road to town as they left. Had it predicted this? She shuddered more violently. Mabel moved toward her and wrapped her in a hug.

"Are you all right?" she asked gruffly, before pulling back to search Parker's face.

"Yes." Parker had never felt so small, yet so destructive. She wanted them to lock her inside a metal box so she couldn't hurt anyone. She heard light footsteps behind her as Ellie joined them, wrapping her arm around Parker's shoulders. Together, they stared at what she had done.

Mabel was looking worriedly at George, who was leaning heavily against the truck.

"Well," George said through labored breaths. "It seems, Parker, that you're more powerful than we realized."

Mabel let out a short laugh. "I certainly don't want to get on your bad side again. Parker, we'll need you to clean up this mess."

CHAPTER FOURTEEN

The rock had broken off the hillside and tumbled directly into their path. Ellie had seen it all. Mabel had seen it too, and just in time. Now they were sitting on the hood of the truck, thanking their lucky stars (Mabel's phrasing) that another car hadn't come along. The rock was too big to move aside, and rather than calling for help, Mabel and George were using the opportunity to teach the girls a lesson in self-control.

Of course, Ellie knew that not everyone could talk to animals and that her ability to understand Arlo, Toffee, Walter, and the others—and George's ability to heal them—was unique.

It was something different to think of it as a power she could harness and control.

Ellie looked at Parker, who was staring intently at Mabel.

"As we explained previously, many of our family members were given a gift." George crossed his arms over his chest. "Some of us can communicate with creatures and plants. Some of us have the power of cold and the rain. Some of us have the power of fire, an ability to raise tremors from the earth. It's different for everyone who's gifted."

George nodded at Mabel. "Show them."

Mabel closed her eyes. Suddenly a cold wind cut through the heavy mountain fog. It wrapped itself around Mabel. To Ellie, it looked like a ribbon of icy glitter that spun around her aunt's feet, her waist, and her hands.

Like her own personal hurricane.

"So it's like," Parker said, squeezing her hands tightly. "Like, our whole family?"

"Not everyone, but someone in every generation of our family as far as we can trace our ancestry."

Ellie tried to imagine her mother with her own personal hurricane. Or maybe she could make the ground shake. Mabel paused, looking pained.

"I owe you both an apology for the way I spoke to you earlier. Just because you're kids doesn't mean you deserve less than our full respect. And clearly you *are* ready to know more."

"Parker," George chimed in, "what's different about you is that you seem to have multiple gifts—the ability to produce light and manipulate the earth's surface matter. Most of us only have one. Your mother had many, but she was highly unusual. It's why she traveled so much—she was exceptionally good at what she did, and so a lot of people needed her. Ellie, it's possible you may have more too; we'll know in time."

Ellie nodded. She wasn't envious of Parker. She thought it would be difficult to have more. Talking to animals was already more than she could handle. Sometimes Walter's thoughts crowded her brain when she was trying to sleep at night, and he wasn't especially interesting.

Parker looked at the ground. "What does this mean? What do we do now?"

"It means the same thing any power means," Mabel said. "It means you both have a responsibility, in this case, to learn how to use and control your powers. You'll learn to help one another harness and direct them. In our family, two fight as one. And Parker, your powers are very strong, and they're only just emerging. It's important for you not to let them control you."

"So we might become even more powerful?" Parker asked quietly.

Mabel frowned. "You might. You likely will. But we are here to give back. It's not about obtaining more power; it's about understanding how to wield it."

"But . . ." Ellie heard a tremor in her sister's voice and saw her eyes beginning to well. "I want to go home."

Ellie could feel the pain pouring off her sister.

Mabel dropped her hands. "Parker," she said, "I don't think you understand. This is who you are."

It took an hour for Parker to learn how to shatter the large rock into pieces small enough for them to clear from the road. Two cars drove by in that time, and both asked if they needed help.

"We've got someone coming!" Mabel answered brightly each time. Then Ellie watched her sister resume her focus. It seemed as though Parker had to channel all her anxious energy—the restlessness she had thrown into sports in Harborville—into a concentrated force within her. Whenever Parker became frustrated, Ellie absorbed some of it, pulling it deep within her to relieve Parker's burden, until Parker calmed down and refocused. By the time they were done, she was exhausted.

"OK, on to the market," George said cheerfully. "Parker, you were incredible. You too, Ellie."

"Me?" Ellie was confused. "What did I do?"

"You forget that I can sense feelings too. I saw you shouldering part of Parker's burden so she could be free to complete her task."

"You did?" Parker looked at Ellie with wonder. "I felt that. I didn't know it was you."

"I didn't know it was special," Ellie told them. "It's just something that's easy to do."

"No, no. That's part of your gift. You have to be careful with it, Ellie. If you shoulder too much of other people's pain, you could wind up hurting yourself."

Ellie nodded. All her life, she had been able to see how people were feeling, sometimes even before they saw it themselves. Especially Parker. Only recently, though, did she feel as though she could simply lift the hurt from other people and hold it for a while.

"Are we really still going to the market?" Parker asked. "After all that?"

"Sure." Mabel grinned. "We promised you ice cream, didn't we?"

"Mmm," Ellie said. "Chocolate with peanut butter chunks for me, please." She knew Parker was tired, but it would be good for them to do something different. And besides, she didn't want the day to end. She felt closer to Mabel and George now that they'd shared so much.

"Rainbow sherbet for me," George said, sliding back into the front passenger seat. Ellie didn't miss how he winced when he reached back to grab the seat belt. Maybe the jolt from the swerve hadn't completely spared him.

"Oh!" Ellie gasped when they turned onto Main Street in the town of Bearsted less than ten minutes later. "It's so sweet."

"Not bad," Parker allowed, grinning.

While Harborville was large and sprawling, with chain stores and supermarkets, Bearsted was compact and charming. It looked like a town that might belong near a dollhouse, Ellie thought. All the buildings on Main Street were connected, and each was painted a cheerful color and standing proudly at two stories high. As they searched for a parking spot, they passed a yarn store, two bakeries, a jewelry repair shop, a community center, a vintage clothing boutique, a post office, several restaurants, and a record store.

"It's packed," Parker exclaimed, pressing her nose to the window. "But why didn't we see more cars on the road?"

"Most people come in from outside of town. Weekenders," Mabel explained. "And a lot of people walk in."

"Also, we took a quiet road on purpose," George told them. "What!" He looked at Mabel. "We said no more secrets."

Mabel cut the engine and held up her hands. "I didn't say anything! It's true; we were being cautious. The park over there is where the farmers market is," she said, pointing at a patch of green that was dotted with small tents. "Once we walk over there, you'll be able to see the mountain line. It's quite the view. Oh, and the library is just two blocks east." She pointed in the direction of a small church. "Turn right at the corner and you'll see it on your left."

Ellie slid out of the car, and Parker followed. Mabel and George were doing the thing where they talked with their eyes, she noticed. Parker noticed too; she looked at Ellie and laughed.

"Why don't you girls explore?" George suggested.

"Yes. Explore." Mabel agreed to the suggestion with obvious effort. "But be careful."

"Really?!" Ellie said. "On our own?"

"Sure," Mabel said. "We trust you. Just stick together. We'll handle the rhubarb. And let's meet back here in an hour for ice cream." She looked skyward. "I don't trust the storm to hold off longer than that. You have your cell phones for the time?"

"I do," Parker said. "But I'm really good at telling time without it. It's my superpower."

"Seriously, Parker?" Ellie said. "Another one? Now you're just being smug."

Parker grinned. "First stop, Internet!" she shouted, holding her fist aloft.

It took a few minutes for them to locate the two-story building that served as Bearsted's library, because it looked more like an old Victorian house than a library. It was painted robin's-egg blue. They entered through a white picket fence and ascended the stairs to a front porch lined in wicker furniture. A couple about their dad's age was seated in the wicker loveseat, reading to a little boy. A rolling cart housing stacks of old, dusty paperbacks was marked with a sign that read $1 each. The door to the building was propped open, and if Ellie hadn't seen the simple sign hanging at the gate that read, Bearsted Library, 8–6, she probably would have thought they were trespassing.

"Smells like old people," Parker commented, wrinkling her nose. "I'm going to find the computer." She took off toward the back rooms, scanning quickly as she went. Ellie felt herself smile a little. Typical Parker, always in motion, never wasting a minute. With Parker gone, Ellie scanned her surroundings with interest. The room was empty of people, which was frankly how Ellie preferred it. Every single wall was covered in rows and rows of books, with several bookshelves set up in the middle of each room and cozy, threadbare armchairs wedged in the corners.

It felt homey inside, the way she'd imagined Haven House looking. She faced a broad wooden staircase to the second floor; a small room with a fireplace and deep mauve ceilings was to her right and a large room with a massive crystal chandelier was on her left. Ellie supposed it had once been a parlor; she half expected a plate of sugar cookies and a pot of tea to materialize on the windowsill. In the corner of the room was a large, antique bird cage and inside it were two chirping birds.

Ellie moved toward that room, intending to talk to the birds. When she approached, though, the orange canary ruffled its feathers and squawked. *Not again,* she felt it saying to its friend, a red-and-gray cockatoo. *If another child wedges a grimy finger into our house, I swear I'll eat it for supper.*

Ellie put her hands on her hips, miffed. "I'm not a child," she informed the bird. "I've just turned twelve! And I'd take a look at those filthy talons of yours before you go calling someone else grimy." Ellie brushed past the cage but saw the cockatoo's beak open slightly and its leg lift so it could inspect its talons.

After that, Ellie wandered aimlessly, looking for anything to read and finding nothing very interesting besides several old *Archie* digests and a faded *Nancy Drew.* She was rooting through a pile of dusty magazines when she heard someone chuckling.

"Looking for something to read?"

Ellie spun around to find a stranger lurking behind her. The woman was strikingly tall like George, with tight brown curls piled on top of her head and stuck in place with a series of sparkly combs and clips. She wore a floor-length orange dress and a crisp tailored jacket the color of cement. Unlike Mabel and George, this woman's whole face was a study in vibrant color from her bright pink lips to the purple glitter ringing her brown eyes under the thick glass of gold-rimmed frames.

"Good luck finding anything published after the seventies." The woman chuckled.

"Oh," Ellie said, looking at an August 1958 issue of *Better Homes and Gardens,* which she was clutching like a life preserver. She squinted, dazzled by the woman's presence. "Yeah, I guess it's kind of a lost cause."

"Finding something to read is? Not at all." The woman smiled, beckoning Ellie with a curled finger. "Follow me."

Ellie froze. "Um. I should find my twin sister."

"Oh!" The woman smiled and offered Ellie her hand. It was pleasingly cool in Ellie's own, and their linked hands reminded Ellie of a yin and yang symbol: two contrasting things forming a harmonious whole. She retrieved her hand. All that talk about balance was sinking in, apparently.

"Sorry. So rude. I'm Ms. Boudin, the librarian. It's just around the corner. And if your sister is the tall, fair brunette around your same age who's been parked in front of the computer for fifteen minutes, then I can show you where she is as well."

"That sounds like her," Ellie replied, smiling. "She's been dying without the Internet. I'm Ellie."

"You two are staying up at Haven House, aren't you?"

Ellie felt a shiver of discomfort travel up her spine. "How did you know that?"

"Oh, small town, people talk," Ms. Boudin said. "Apparently your aunt and uncle don't come back much, so it's quite the hot goss when they do. And having you two in tow got people's tongues wagging. Being a librarian is like being a bartender, sweetie. Bad comparison—you wouldn't know. What I mean is, I hear everything. Come on, then."

Ms. Boudin pivoted like a dancer on her yellow suede heels, and Ellie felt herself following. The next inner room of the library was outfitted much the same as the front room. Aside from shelves and shelves of books, the only other objects that occupied the space were a standing desk in the center of the room and a set of big, puffy yellow chairs that looked like slabs of butter stationed against the walls.

Ellie looked at her phone. She didn't want George and Mabel to worry.

"So, I'm somewhat new at this gig," Ms. Boudin noted. "But I brought a number of things with me when I moved in—I'd heard the collection here was rather fusty. I keep the good stuff back here, behind my desk. We should be able to find you something you'll like. What's your pleasure? Fantasy? Mystery?"

"Um." Ellie blushed. "Do you have any Polly Marker romance novels?"

"*Do I?* You bet!" Ms. Boudin ducked low and riffled around behind her desk while Ellie waited, politely scanning her surroundings so as not to seem impatient.

"No . . . not this. No . . . ah! Here we go." She popped back up and triumphantly handed Ellie a slim volume.

"Have you read this one?"

"No!" Ellie gasped, delighted. "Doesn't this one come out next month? How did you get it so early?"

"Magic," she said with a wink. "I have friends in book places. I'll let you know if I get anything new in if you leave me your number." Ms. Boudin slid a pen toward her.

"Sure." Ellie nodded. She fished in her back pocket for something to write her number on and pulled out a scrap of paper. She unfolded it halfway before realizing what it was.

"Gemini," Ms. Boudin said, staring at the scrap. "Oops! Sorry, didn't mean to peek. Is that a note from your sister? How sweet."

"No." Ellie hastily stuffed Sadie's note to her mom back in her pocket.

"Oh!" Ms. Boudin looked confused. "Never mind, then. Anyway, I've got paper right here."

She reached under her desk for a pad of paper and pushed it in Ellie's direction. Ellie hesitated, but as there were three other names and numbers already jotted on the pad, she figured informality was just the way of things here. She jotted her digits, pausing when she realized it was useless.

"I just remembered—I don't really get a signal," she told the librarian.

"Oh. Right." Ms. Boudin nodded, handing the book to Parker. "I'd heard Haven was a little old-fashioned that way. How are you finding things there? Beautiful view, from what I hear."

"It's nice," Ellie replied, turning the book over in her hands. "We've had some friendly animals come in, and there's a dog I like a lot. He's quite intelligent. Always has something interesting to say."

Ms. Boudin laughed, and Ellie realized her mistake. "Uh. He doesn't really talk. I only mean—"

"I always wished my cat could talk," Ms. Boudin replied. "But I suspect it would be a series of complaints. *Why must I suffer dry food? This chair is lumpy. Make the sun shine* all *day. How'd I get stuck with this lady?*"

"Oh no!" Ellie gushed, surprising herself. "I'm sure your cat is delighted to live with you."

Thankfully, Ms. Boudin seemed to take this line of discussion in stride.

"Well," she said. "Now you'll have a delightful book to keep you company when the dog you like is busy. Shall I take you to your sister? Assuming she's still hunkered down in front of that infernal machine, that is."

Ellie nodded. She was beginning to like Ms. Boudin. She was odd, but on the good side of odd. They walked over a faded red runner through a narrow corridor, Ms. Boudin's yellow heels sinking deep into the thick carpet pile.

"My, my. I would have worn my hiking boots had I known you were coming," she joked. "Maybe it's silly that I get dressed for work at a job where I hardly see anyone."

"I don't think so. Not at all." Ellie's felt herself relaxing into the conversation, especially since Ms. Boudin was walking ahead of her rather than making scary eye contact. "I think it's very nice that you set a standard for yourself." The hallway was long, Ellie realized. It seemed longer than the house.

"And do *you*, Ellie? Set a standard for yourself?" Ms. Boudin stopped at the hallway's end and turned to face her. Ellie avoided her eyes.

"I think so," she said.

"I think so too," Ms. Boudin agreed. "I can tell just by looking at you. Now make sure you believe in it too. And in yourself." Ellie pondered this as Ms. Boudin stepped aside, urging her forward.

Ellie gasped. After the dark of the corridor, this back room—which was a closed-in porch with floor-to-ceiling windows, facing a garden—was blinding. Ellie heard a clap of thunder sound overhead. So Mabel and George were right; it was going to storm.

"There she is," Ms. Boudin said brightly.

Sure enough, as soon as Ellie's vision adjusted, she saw Parker perched at a long, wooden table lining the wall opposite. She was so immersed in whatever she was doing, she hadn't noticed them enter. In front of her was a giant beige box, some relic from a bygone era.

"Is that a *computer*?" Ellie asked.

"Oh!" Parker finally noticed them and swiveled in her wooden chair. "That's exactly what *I* said. Isn't it crazy? They don't even have Wi-Fi here. It's something called 'dial-down.'"

"Dial-up," Ms. Boudin corrected. "I tried to have that updated, but apparently it isn't possible due to the fact that this is a historically preserved building. Connectivity in Bearsted is about twenty years behind the times, though, so it probably doesn't make a difference either way. I think this ancient desktop was the former librarian's mother's. It works, but it's very slow."

"A little wheel spins even when I just try to *type*," Parker complained. "And there must be something wrong with it, because it didn't load any new mail for me." She sounded grouchy. "It isn't possible that Clara wouldn't have tried to reach out through email when she couldn't get me on text. My dumb phone still only has one bar even in town." She glanced at her phone as if to confirm she hadn't missed anything.

Ellie and Ms. Boudin exchanged a look. "Do you want to—"

But since Parker already knew exactly what she wanted to do—or say—and to whom, she turned back to the gargantuan machine, her fingers flying over its crunchy keyboard.

"Well," Ms. Boudin shrugged. "If you two ever need a place to come and be, the library isn't always open, but it's *often* open."

Ellie looked over her sister's shoulder. She had an email half composed and was dashing off the end.

Clara!

I'm in BEARSTED and it's a NIGHTMARE! I can't even use my phone at all, even in town apparently, so I have no idea if you're even texting me or what? There's NOTHING here and I'm freaking out! I'm writing on a dinosaur at the library! I AM SO BORED but I have THE COOLEST secret I have to tell you!!!!!

Please please please email me back or call me or I guess I'll call you from the landline?

UGH.

Ok I love you and I'll talk to you soon!

P

Ellie drew back from the computer just as Parker clicked "send." Her face burned, and she avoided Ms. Boudin's eyes. How could Parker be bored, when so much was going on around them? Why wasn't Ellie enough company for Parker? And what was the secret? Was she going to tell Clara about their powers?! Ellie's thoughts were turning dark when she heard the echo of a horn honking. A truck horn. Mabel and George.

"Gah!" Parker clicked "send" several more times. "Why is nothing working?!" Ellie noticed her face getting pink.

Ms. Boudin shifted beside Ellie. "I think someone's waiting for you outside," she said. "Parker, if you trust me with it, I can make sure your note sends, and I can log you out after."

The horn honked again, long and hard. "I thought we were meeting them back at the market," Parker grumbled.

"They must have finished up." Ellie shifted uncomfortably. "It looks like the storm started." She gestured out at the windows. Beyond them, the rain was coming down in sheets. We'd better go if we want them to trust us to explore on our own again."

"OK, OK." Parker stood up like a shot, almost knocking Ms. Boudin over. Then she bolted out of the library, leaving Ellie in the dust. Some twin.

"Ms. Boudin," Ellie remembered, just as she was moving

toward the door. "What did you mean, 'Gemini'?" Ms. Boudin looked blank. "Earlier, when you saw my note."

"Oh! Just that I saw the symbol for the astrological sign. Two straight parallel lines intersecting with two curved lines at top and bottom. That's Gemini—twins. Two parts of the same whole. Right? That's why I assumed it was a note from your sister. Two is the magic number!"

"Oh." Ellie's face flamed. "Right. Thanks! Nice to meet you!" Then she darted down the corridor behind Parker.

"Nice to meet you too! That's due back in a week," Ms. Boudin called after her. "I'll try calling you if we get any more Polly Marker books!"

Outside, Parker was already in the truck and buckled up, glaring out the window. Mabel gave Ellie a stern look but didn't say anything. George handed her an apricot.

"Sorry," Ellie said, even though she hadn't done anything wrong. She was glad she had the book for evidence that she had been doing normal library things and nothing nefarious, though she had never done anything nefarious in her life unless you counted peeking at Parker's journal. Ellie turned over in her head what Ms. Boudin had said about the Gemini symbol. If two was the magic number—if Ellie and Parker together were magic—why couldn't Parker see it?

"Why did you pick us up?" Ellie asked Aunt Mabel and George. She folded her arms over her chest. "Is it because of the weather?" The wind had picked up, and the rain had started coming down in sheets. Bits of paper and debris blew down the street and swirled around bushes and trees. Flower stalks bent so far sideways, Ellie feared they'd snap.

"You could say that," Mabel allowed. Ellie saw George place a hand on Mabel's arm, as if to calm her.

"We already mentioned this to Parker, but there was an accident at the market," George explained. "One of the tents was struck by lightning. Came out of nowhere. The whole market shut down."

"Oh no!" Ellie gasped. "That's awful. Was anyone hurt?"

"Everyone is fine except for about fifty pounds' worth of asparagus," Mabel told them. "Unless you like yours extra-charred." Parker was still sitting stiffly, her eyes glued to the sidewalk flashing by outside her window.

"It is odd, the timing of it," Mabel said casually. "Wouldn't you say, Parker? I was hoping you'd have a little more self-control after the incident this morning."

Parker finally reacted.

"I didn't do it!" she shouted. "I already told you! I was emailing Clara."

Ellie looked at Parker with concern. She was so upset she was trembling, which was unusual for Parker, who typically didn't let anyone get to her easily. Had she really sent a lightning bolt through a tent because she was so upset she hadn't heard from Clara?

"Now Parker," George said worriedly. "We know you didn't *mean* to do it—" Mabel snorted at this—"but staying in control of your emotions is essential to controlling your powers. I don't think you realize the extent of your gifts, dear."

"I'm telling you! I know when I do things because I feel all . . . *tingly and weird,*" Parker said, raising her voice. "I didn't feel that way at the library! It wasn't me."

"Maybe it was just the weather," Ellie suggested.

"None of this is normal, Ellie. Someone is making it happen, which means someone is letting the Danger get closer. If not Parker, then I don't know who." Mabel's lips were a flat line. Ellie had never seen her so frustrated.

Ellie looked at Parker. She wished she could communicate with her sister the way she could communicate with Arlo or Walter or those birds at the library.

I know you didn't do it, she thought hard, hoping Parker would read her words in her eyes. *I believe you.* She wasn't sure if Parker got the message, so she reached over and squeezed her hand, just in case. For the first time all afternoon, Parker offered her a small smile.

Ellie didn't like what was going on. Aunt Mabel and George were doing that thing where they thought they knew best just because they were adults. But they weren't listening. Not at all. The truck pulled onto Main Street and headed toward the long, winding country road that led back to Haven. Café owners were pulling their outdoor seating inside and rolling back awnings. Napkins and menus blew across the road, and the rain pushed harder, slanting toward them.

Two figures of similar height in hoodies and jeans, holding identical, clear, polka-dot umbrellas hurried down the sidewalk with their heads down. Black braids peeked out of one of the hoodies. Something about the way they moved looked familiar to Ellie. She straightened, squinting as the truck drove past. Then she turned and rubbed the fog from the window, peering back to get a glimpse of their features.

For a second, she could have sworn she knew the pair. She could have sworn the long braids belonged to Cassie Phillips, and the owner of the other polka-dot umbrella was her brother, Casey. But that didn't make sense. It made no sense at all. She turned back to Parker, and found her sister staring at her, her face grim. Parker raised her eyebrows as if to communicate something.

Ellie listened hard.

I saw them too, Parker said without speaking.

The gate was open when they pulled in the drive, skidding through mounting puddles. Felix's car was parked at Haven

House. But that wasn't the alarming thing. The alarming thing was the sound of Arlo's frantic barks.

"Now what is this?" Mabel said aloud, pulling up beside Felix's car and shifting the truck into park. "My goodness gracious."

They all jumped out of the car and moved quickly in the direction of the sound, each of them immediately soaked to the skin from the driving rain. As soon as they cleared the front of the house and had a view of the barn, Ellie saw it—or rather, *them*. There were animals everywhere. They were too far away to see through the rain what *kind* of animals, but Arlo was making frantic efforts to herd them into the barn and was having a hard time of it—that much was clear.

"Felix!" George shouted. "What's going on? Mabel, you and Parker go back to the house and make sure the windows are shut. Ellie and I will take care of this."

The closer they got to the barn, the more Ellie's head filled with the frantic whimpers and bleats and mewls of injured animals. First, the noise. Then Ellie felt it: pain shimmering through every end of her body, until she was doubled over with it. *It was hard to imagine anyone surviving this sort of agony*, she thought as George turned back to her.

"Ellie," George cried, "You can do this. Focus through the pain."

Why am I so weak? Ellie wondered. Why couldn't she be as strong as Parker? She took a step forward, gritting her teeth. Pain flooded her right calf muscle and spread up to her thigh. It made her heart thud so fast she thought she might pass out. Then she heard the voices.

Help, please, they said, each in their unique way. *You're our only hope.*

Ellie found a part of herself that was remote. It was deep inside her and separate from her physical self. She concentrated hard on putting all her pain in that spot. She poured it into the little dark place and imagined shutting a door on it. She knew she'd have to let it out later. But for now, she'd lock it up inside to survive.

Ellie pressed on. *Believe in it,* she told herself, remembering Boudin's words.

When she got to the barn, aching and breathless and feeling like she'd just run a marathon instead of walked across half an acre, Arlo had just finished herding the animals inside. George and Felix were staring, wide-eyed, at the chaos surrounding them. Arlo was panting heavily.

"Oh, Felix, this is awful," George said. "I don't know where to begin."

Ellie took it in, Arlo at her side. There were no fewer than two dozen woodland creatures: deer, squirrels, a fox, a couple of badgers. A wolf. He met Ellie's eyes, his own pleading.

I won't hurt you, he choked out between labored breaths. Ellie could see a deep gash between his ribs—his blood pooled beneath him. *Please.* Ellie drew a breath, letting down her guard. The door to the dark place opened a crack. A searing pain filled the left side of her body, where her own ribs were. Ellie pushed it back, back, back with all her might, until it was wedged all the way in, and the door firmly shut once more. The pain clamored against it, a dim echo filling her. She had to concentrate. She had to help.

"Is that a—" Felix sounded frightened.

"Yes," George said. "Yes. And that means a predator more powerful than that wolf was after them."

"They had to have hopped the wall," Ellie said wonderingly.

Wouldn't you? Arlo asked, *if something very big and powerful and frightening were trying to take your life?*

Ellie rested a hand on her friend's head.

And then she got to work.

CHAPTER FIFTEEN

"**P**arker!"

The insistent voice of the sofa didn't come from where she'd have guessed, a thing Parker found interesting. *If* a sofa were to talk, she'd have assumed a big fluffy sofa like this one would lift a cushion to form a mouth that could open and close. It turned out that wasn't true at all.

The sofa spoke through one of its wooden legs. It was hard to see if the leg had a mouth or not.

From her beanbag chair, Parker crawled over so she could investigate the leg. She shook her head. Talking sofas! Haven House was truly bonkers.

"Parker!" the sofa said again. She peered at the leg. No mouth, but there was something tiny moving in the wood grain. A bug? Wasn't it *Ellie* who was supposed to be able to talk to animals? Did that ability extend to insects? Parker wasn't sure.

"What do you want?" Parker said.

The fine dark etchings of the wood grain trembled. "It's time to melt us cut up the corn Lindas."

Parker leaned in close, so that her nose was practically touching the sofa leg. Her eyes crossed trying to make sense of the little, shivering, speaking presence. The world went blurry.

"What?"

Exasperated, the sofa raised its voice. "The corn Lindas!"

The world began to un-blur. Parker swam up out of sleep, left the dream behind, and woke in her bedroom at Haven. Edges sharpened and her sleepy eyes focused on Mabel, who was gently shaking her awake. Ellie was at Mabel's side, already dressed and looking irritatingly chipper and alert.

"It's time to help us put up the storm windows," Mabel said.

"Oh." Parker blinked. "That sofa was hard to understand."

Ellie giggled. Mabel frowned. "What sofa?"

Parker sat up and rubbed her eyes. "Never mind."

"It's getting bad out there again," Ellie said. "You know what's weird? I could have sworn I saw snow flurries."

Mabel turned and slid aside the patchwork curtains, fashioned from old cardigans. Parker's breath caught in her throat. Outside, the morning sky was shot through with wisps of fast-moving, charcoal-colored clouds that flowed like lava. Dry leaves and clumps of dirt swirled in a madcap dance across the barn roof. In the forest beyond, trees swayed and bent ungracefully toward the earth. Atop the lonely hills far beyond the stone wall that bordered Haven, a bolt of lightning stabbed a dark farmhouse.

Parker's palms tingled. The underside of her tongue buzzed with electrical urgency. "I thought we were safe here."

"We are," Mabel assured her. "But like I said yesterday, the Danger is getting very close. Between the farmers market and afterward, here, with those poor animals—I've never seen it this bad before." Mabel looked distinctly agitated. She clasped her hands in front of her overalls, then unclasped them and hooked her thumbs around the edges of her pockets. Mabel's reaction frightened Parker. After all, this was a woman who only yesterday had cloaked herself in her own personal hurricane.

Choose strong, Parker. "What can we do?"

"Why don't you get up and get dressed, to start. You can take George some toast and tea when you're ready. He isn't feeling well after last night; I think the animals really did a number on him. I told him to rest. Then you and Ellie can eat and after that, we'll do the windows."

"OK," Parker said carefully. She knew Mabel still blamed her for the chaos at the farmers market—the swelling, gusting winds; the tent burnt to smithereens, the unfortunate situation with the asparagus—but surely Mabel knew that the animals, at least, weren't her doing.

Unless . . . In the same way her out-of-control powers *could theoretically have* called forth the storm that trashed the market, could they also have summoned a vicious beast to the edge of Haven?

All those voices. All that pain. Screaming through her sister's mind. Ellie had told her everything, along with the fact that George had been so weak midway through healing the animals that he'd passed out—and that's when Ellie had stepped in and discovered she could heal animals too. Oh, and Felix had seen the whole thing.

Parker wished she could go back to sleep. Rejoin the dream in progress, curl up on the talking sofa. Be alone.

Ellie turned to Mabel. "I'm sorry I'm not as strong as Parker is. Maybe I could have helped balance things out a little bit."

"That's all right, Ellie. We all must develop at our own pace. It's the best way. The *only* way." Mabel smiled. "After all, it's why you're here." Parker thought she looked sad. "Meet me downstairs by the fireplace after you've eaten, OK? We'll start with the ground floor windows and work our way up."

With that, Mabel left Parker alone with her sister.

Ellie glanced over her shoulder. Together they listened as Mabel's footsteps receded down the hall.

"You didn't say anything, did you?" Ellie whispered, settling cross-legged on the end of Parker's bed.

"That you can heal animals and Felix knows and George told you not to tell Mabel?"

"Shhhh!" Ellie's eyes widened.

"Of course not! Who would I have told? I haven't seen anyone besides you and Mabel just now."

"OK. I just . . . George's not doing well this morning. I'm worried."

"I'm sure he just needs some rest," Parker said doubtfully. "Why do you think he told you not to mention your healing to Mabel?" Parker asked. George and Mabel shared everything—it didn't make sense.

"He said Mabel might get stressed out if she thought the animal thing had something to do with my powers," Ellie said quietly. "That Mabel might worry that you and I both have powers we can't control, and he doesn't want her to get worked up."

"I know you didn't do it, Ellie," Parker told her.

"Thanks. I know you didn't do the thing at the market."

"Thanks."

"I'm not saying it because you said that to me—I'm saying it because it's obviously true."

"This place makes it pretty hard to figure out what's true and what's not."

"Remember the weather vanes?" Ellie said suddenly.

"Yeah. What about them?"

"The one with the lion was pointing toward the woods yesterday before we left. The one with the earth symbol was pointing toward town."

Parker hesitated. "That was probably a coincidence," she said finally.

"I don't know." Ellie bit her thumbnail. "Maybe . . . but those weather vanes never worked at all before we came to Haven. They didn't spin *ever* in Harborville. We thought they were broken. Remember?"

"Yeah."

Ellie was right. It was very strange that the weather vanes had all of a sudden started spinning in specific directions now that they were at Haven.

"There's another thing . . ." Ellie trailed off. Then she put her hand over her mouth to stifle a laugh.

"What?" Parker took a long swig of water from a glass on her copper-wire nightstand.

Arlo nosed into the room, sauntered over to the bed, leapt up onto Parker's pillow, and proceeded to lazily nibble at his paws.

"Ah," Parker said, glancing between Arlo and Ellie. "Inside joke?"

Arlo showed his teeth, stretching his gums back, and closed his eyes.

"What's the other thing?" Parker asked impatiently. "Ellie, hurry and tell me. I've got to get dressed and get George his toast." Parker tossed her sweaty sheets aside—one had been twined around her leg—and went to her closet to grab a fresh pair of overalls. (Was she actually getting *used* to wearing these things?)

"So, do you remember that note I found from Mom's friend Sadie?" Parker could tell Ellie was choosing her words carefully. "The one that was in the photo box."

"Of course I do. What about it?"

"Right. Well." She shook her head. "I don't know if you remember the little symbol she drew in her sign-off? The curvy lines with straight lines?"

"I don't, but you can show me later." Parker was getting impatient. "Get to the point, Ellie. I don't want us to get in trouble after yesterday."

"Ms. Boudin at the library said the sign stands for Gemini."

Parker gave her sister a blank look and resumed pulling on a pair of socks.

"Gemini is the twin constellation," Ellie explained. Parker still didn't know what she was getting at. "It's the star symbol for twins," Ellie went on.

"And . . ."

"And," Ellie said, "Sadie used it in her note to Mom! Think about it."

"Are you saying Mom and Sadie used the twins symbol because they were twins? That's impossible!" Parker choked back a laugh. "Sorry, Ellie, but Mom didn't have a sister. We would have known, don't you think?"

"Maybe," Ellie said casually. "Or maybe not, if there was a good reason to hide it."

"Ellie McFadden!" Parker was shocked and delighted. "I didn't know your brain was even capable of going somewhere so sinister."

Ellie picked a pillow up off the bed and threw it at Parker.

"Seriously! Do you think Mabel and George have been lying to us about Mom being an only child?"

"That would mean Mom and Dad lied to us our whole lives too," Parker reminded her. "You think both of them just forgot to mention Mom's sister for twelve years straight?"

Ellie raised her eyebrows. Apparently, she did think that. Parker thought for a moment. "It doesn't make sense. Why hide it, if Mom really had a sister? Like, what's the big deal?"

As they talked, Parker felt a peculiar energy course through her that had nothing to do with her powers. It was purely a result of Parker and Ellie against the world—sisters, working together, leaving petty slights behind, forming a bulwark against the twisting, shadowy world of adults and their secret agendas. A world that even their dad had known about and hidden from them.

"I don't know," Ellie admitted in a low voice. "But it *is* a little odd, don't you think?

Parker knew she could count on her sister's sensitivity to properly explain any situation—and tease out the truth. This deep and honest sense of things had been Ellie's gift long before her newfound powers appeared.

All Parker had to do was trust her sister.

She found that it came naturally. And it felt good.

"So how do we find out for sure?" Parker asked. "Is there anyone in town who would know the answers?"

"Like someone who was around when Mom was little? A friend of George's and Mabel's? I don't know. That's a good thought, but wouldn't it get back to them? And besides, Mom was only here occasionally, right?"

"How about Felix's grandpa, Ray?" Parker clapped. It was genius. "He'd definitely know."

"But we don't know whether they can be trusted," Ellie reminded her.

Parker drew back, impressed. "My, my," she said to her sister. "You really *do* have a dark side."

"What was that?" Ellie turned to Arlo. "Oh! Oh really? Maybe . . ."

"What?" It was so annoying when Ellie talked privately to Arlo, who had hopped down onto the floor to nip lightly at Ellie's ankles and calves.

"So," Ellie said to Parker, "Arlo says there's this turtle."

"Seriously? Is this gonna be a bunch of animal gossip?"

"No, I mean, a really *old* turtle. He has apparently lived in the pond at Haven for more than fifty years. He's legendary."

"Can you speak turtle? Can Arlo?"

"Arlo says he can't, and I don't know if I can, but it's worth a try."

Parker headed for the door. "Then let's go."

Ellie hesitated. "There's just one problem. The turtle lives in a pond on the other side of the stone wall. In the forest. Arlo said he would have suggested it sooner, but—"

Arlo stretched. And whined. And got up and walked in a circle.

Parker glanced outside. A branch went sailing past the window. "It might be our only chance to get a straight answer about this. I say we go for it. Right now. Before we're missed."

Ellie nodded. "Just one question before we head out. Who are the Corn Lindas?"

Sneaking out under Mabel's nose wasn't very hard, given the strange architecture of Haven House. With Arlo as their guide, all Parker and Ellie had to do was cut through a mossy tunnel on the third floor, shimmy down an awkwardly sloping passage, and climb out the trunk of a rusty old Chevy pickup. Then it was simply a matter of negotiating a ladder that looked as if it had once belonged in a swimming pool, into a room that had apparently been long-neglected and could only be described as "fuzzy." From there, a swinging saloon door deposited them into the backyard.

"Huh," Parker said. "I'm not sure why we've been going out the front all this time."

The second she stepped out into the tall grass, the wind tried to push Parker back inside. Ellie yelled something from three feet away but the howling, swirling din swallowed up her words.

Arlo bounded ahead. Parker looked at her sister, shrugged, and made herself as low as possible. Running as fast as she could in a half crouch, she followed the speedy cattle dog across the field that surrounded Haven House.

The wind coaxed tears from her eyes and smeared them back across her cheeks. She tried to keep an eye on Arlo and her sister so that she wouldn't give in to the urge to glance up at that terrible sky, but it unfurled to blanket the world so far in every direction, it was impossible not to see. Its deep blue ink was somehow lush and sad at the same time. Meanwhile those charcoal clouds slid across it all, low and uncaring, in pursuit of some path far beyond her understanding.

Parker resisted the urge to look back. If Mabel had spotted them through a window, there would be nothing she could do about it now except keep going.

"Gah!" she shouted as a heavy droplet splattered into her eye. In a matter of seconds, she was soaked. The stone wall, wet and shiny, was just ahead. Through a blur of rain and tears, she watched Arlo scamper easily over it and disappear into the dark forest beyond. She couldn't believe she was back here. She stared, suddenly paralyzed.

"Come on!" Ellie shouted back at Parker. Arlo had disappeared into the brush.

Would Arlo know to stop and wait for them? Even given his obvious intelligence, he was still a cattle dog at heart. Setting him free into a field and over a wall into a forest was like releasing the plunger that sent the pinball rocketing through the bumpers and lights.

Parker willed herself to move forward. Ellie turned and reached out just in time to save her from stumbling on a slick patch of grass. At the same time, she caught sight of the soaking meadow they'd just crossed. What must be several football fields away now, Haven House rose from the earth like an overgrown offshoot, sprouting gables and rooftops in every direction.

Was that tiny dot a face in a window?

"Arlo's waiting for us on the other side," Ellie assured her.

The two sisters paused at the wall. Parker scanned the weather-beaten stones, some jagged and some worn smooth like the ones at the edge of the brook behind their Harborville house. Rain came down in misty curtains. How had she done this before?

"Here we go," Parker said.

"Over the wall," Ellie said.

Choose strong.

Parker placed two hands on a long flat stone and clambered over.

Her feet hit the wet grass on the other side. She was in one piece. Just as before, she hadn't passed through a portal to some netherworld. It was just a stone wall.

Arlo sat there, wagging his tail, looking bemused. A moment later, Ellie was at her side.

Ellie nudged her. "Arlo says, 'remember to breathe.' "

Parker realized she'd been holding her breath. She let it out and took Ellie by the hand as they followed Arlo down an overgrown path—different from the one she'd walked before—into the untamed forest.

The dense canopy of branches and leaves turned the storm's volume down. At first this seemed like a blessing, as the tunnel of stately oaks and gnarled maples kept out the worst of the rain. But after they'd picked their way through a half mile of brambles, roots, and vines—to Arlo's increasing impatience—the weird evasiveness of the storm started to set Parker's nerves on edge. It was uncanny—the howling wind reduced to a stage whisper, battering the treetops, whistling in through gaps in the leaves to tug at strands of Parker's hair . . .

"Um," Ellie said, "Arlo says, 'keep your eyes peeled.'"

"For what?"

A low growl escaped Arlo's throat. His fur rose in spiky clumps along his back. Rain dripped from the trees and made hollow *thwacks* in the mushy loam at their feet.

"*That*," Ellie whispered, gripping Parker's forearm.

The shadow slid like oil across the rough tree trunks. Parker and Ellie stopped short. There was something wrong with the shadow. Light had nothing to do with it. Nothing was casting it. The shadow simply crept of its own accord. And then it was gone.

Your fault.

The whisper slithered into Parker's ears and chilled her mind. She clamped her hands over her ears.

Your fault, your fault, it's all your fault.

"Shut up!" she cried out.

You made your mother leave.

Parker shut her eyes tight. Ellie took her in her arms. "Parker! It's OK! I'm here!"

She didn't want you. She has a better life now.

"SHUT. UP."

Never wanted you.

Never

Never

Parker screamed. A resounding *crack* split the eerie silence of the forest. She opened her eyes as Ellie yanked on her arm, pulling her farther along the overgrown path.

A charred, smoking tree trunk came down on the place she'd just been standing. A black cloud of tiny gnats rose angrily from the forest floor.

Arlo took off. Parker and Ellie crashed through the brush at his heels.

The mocking whisper echoed in Parker's mind. Tears came to her eyes that had nothing to do with the wind.

Suddenly, Arlo stopped short. They'd come to a small clearing where a neat ring of pines bordered a round pond. The surface was placid and still, a sheet of murky glass. Not so much as a ripple interrupted the stillness, despite the wind and rain.

Parker glanced over her shoulder, seeing hints of the shadow everywhere. "Let's talk to this old turtle and get out of here," she said.

Ellie knelt at the edge of the pond and closed her eyes. Arlo rinsed his snout.

A moment later, what appeared to be a small wad of pond scum crawled out of the muck at the edge of the pond. Green, slimy tendrils trailed back into the water. A stench like rotten fish filled the clearing, surprisingly pungent for a creature so small. Ellie scrambled back. Parker covered her nose and mouth. Only Arlo seemed unfazed.

The walking scum kept coming—very slowly. It waddled completely out of the water and only then did it begin to shed its odorous exterior. Which turned out to be algae. As the thing plodded forward and left long strands of wet pond gunk in its wake, a turtle emerged.

A turtle about the size of a salad bowl, with a scarred, ravaged shell.

He took a full minute to look at Arlo, Ellie, and Parker in turn. Then he focused on Ellie and stared at her for a very long time. His face was pinched into a sort of beak that made him look wizened and wrinkled.

"What's he saying?" Parker said.

"He says we can call him Kenneth. He also wants us to know that our odor is distasteful to him."

"Ask him about Mom and Sadie!"

Ellie concentrated. The turtle pulled his head and legs into his shell.

"He has to think," Ellie reported. "He says a lot has happened since he's been here." The shell sat there, motionless.

"For how long?"

"Time is different for turtles," Ellie remarked. Parker suspected she was making that part up. Arlo drank from the pond.

At about the time Parker thought she would explode if she didn't personally knock on Kenneth's shell, his wrinkled old head poked out.

"He says, 'there were two who looked the same,'" Ellie said.

"Two what? Sisters? Mom and somebody else?"

"'Two like you,' he says. He means me." Ellie was silent for a moment, then she nodded at Kenneth.

"What?" Parker asked.

"Kenneth says he's sure of it. That it was a quarter of his life ago and he remembers it clear as day, because no other kids have ventured over the wall since then, and certainly not two who looked the same. He also says it's good manners to bring a caterpillar for him to eat next time. What's with these animals and their snack customs?" The turtle began to slowly retreat backward into the pond.

"Eww." Parker waved. "Thanks, Kenneth. Great meeting you!"

Kenneth slipped fully into the pond and the surface closed over his shell. After a minute, the ripples he'd left in his wake disappeared, and it was as if the turtle had never surfaced.

Parker took a deep breath and let it out. "Two is the magic number."

"Two who looked the same."

"You look just like Mom."

"And Sadie, maybe."

Arlo barked. Oak trees dripped. Parker took Ellie's hand. A dangerous presence swirled around them. The hair rose on Arlo's back, and his ears flattened against his spotted head.

Parker looked at her sister, who was staring at the dog, her expression grave.

"Arlo says we ought to run," Ellie told her.

So they did.

CHAPTER SIXTEEN

It was no use trying to slip back into the house undetected after they returned; Mabel was standing outside watching them cross the field, her overalls bunched at the knees where they met the top of her tall galoshes. She wore a hunter-green raincoat, its hood pulled tight around her face to protect her from the wind and rain. Ellie couldn't make out her features at a distance, but her ramrod-straight posture and two fists that rested squarely on her hips indicated she wasn't happy. Ellie wasn't afraid, though. After what had happened in the woods—after the swirling thing had whispered its vile thoughts as they ran—she thought very little could scare her.

"We can't say anything," Parker told her suddenly, reaching for her hand. "About Sadie, I mean." Arlo yipped twice in agreement.

I wouldn't recommend it either, he advised, then took off running in circles around them, nudging them closer to the house with light nips and barks.

"I don't know," Ellie said, trying to keep her voice loud enough so Parker could hear her over the din of the rain and thunder, but quiet enough that Mabel—only about half a Harborville block length away, now—wouldn't. "I think we ought to ask for the truth."

"Please, let's just think about it first," Parker pleaded. "Say you'll wait, at least until we have a chance to talk through it ourselves. Anyway, what are we going to tell them? That we have it on good authority *from an elderly pond turtle* that Mom and Sadie were identical twins?"

Well, when she put it like that.

"OK." Ellie thought of Parker's journal. Maybe if she played it Parker's way, they'd finally discuss *all* the secrets that had been simmering—not just the one about Sadie.

When they got closer to the house, Mabel grabbed each of them by the wrist and hauled them inside. Arlo slipped in after them and shook his fur vigorously, wetting every surface within three feet.

Luckily, we cattle dogs have rain-resistant coats, he told Ellie, who was shivering in her own soaked clothes. *I'll be dry in a jiff.*

"What is the meaning of this?" Mabel had raised her voice, which put it at about five decibel levels over their dad's version of stern. "What were you two doing running around in the rain? And did I see you climbing over the stone wall just now, or have I hallucinated? Because I could have sworn

I was explicit about you not going into the woods. You could have been killed!"

"Arlo ran off after a squirrel," Parker lied smoothly. "And after what happened with those forest animals, we were worried. So we tried to save him."

It was all a load of bunk (a phrase her dad sometimes used), Ellie knew. Arlo was more equipped to save them than the other way around, and he could run a million times faster than they ever could. But it was plausible enough an excuse for Mabel—a Mabel who underestimated them as kids who did not know any better—to buy.

Mabel crossed her arms over her chest and look from Ellie to Parker and back again.

"Fine," she said grimly. "But don't let it happen again. George has had enough stress already. No need to add this to the mix. Now stay right there before you go ruining the furniture." She walked into the kitchen and retrieved two towels—which looked old and faded but thick and soft—from a drawer next to the sink.

"How is George?" Ellie asked softly. She pulled off her shoes and accepted the towel Mabel offered her. Parker gratefully accepted the other towel and began squeezing out her hair. Mabel sighed, then sat heavily on the stairs to the second floor.

"He's feeling a bit better today. I know he'll want to check on the animals later, Ellie, if you'd like to join him. But he's worried, of course. We heard from your father while you two were gallivanting in the woods."

"What!" Parker leapt to her feet, one sock off, the other leaving a slimy trail on the floor. "Dad called? What did he say?"

"It seems he never made it to the Netherlands. There have been tornadoes all over the Midwest, so he never left California. The weather in Harborville has been awful too, he says."

"Oh no," Ellie whispered. "Did he say when he'll call back?"

Mabel shrugged. "He said he'd try again tomorrow. But Parker, I'm starting to worry. This is starting to look like direct result of the effect your powers have had on Bearsted. If you don't get control of yourself soon, there could be a massive ripple effect. While Ellie's outside with George, why don't you and I practice more techniques for exercising self-control."

Parker nodded miserably. "OK," she agreed.

"How do you know it's Parker?" Ellie asked. For a second the image of two identical, umbrella-wielding figures clad in hoodies and jeans passed through her mind. She hesitated. "What if . . . someone else is making strange things happen?"

"That's ridiculous. We'd know about anyone else in town with gifts like our own."

"But how do you know for sure?" Ellie pressed. She could tell Mabel was feeling unnerved. She shifted from one foot to the next, and her cheeks were turning pink.

"Don't talk about what you don't understand," she snapped. Ellie felt a swell of frustration rise up inside her. "But—"

"Ellie," Parker interrupted softly. "It's OK." She turned to Mabel. "I'd appreciate that," she told their aunt. "I definitely want to figure out how to get myself under control."

"Oh dear," Mabel said softly, stepping forward to wrap Parker in an embrace. "I am so sorry. I didn't mean to snap at you. There's no excuse for that kind of behavior, especially here at Haven." She rested her hands on Parker's shoulders and looked at her long and hard. "Forgive me, both of you. I didn't sleep much last night—George is still very weak, and I didn't want to leave him alone." She hesitated before continuing, as if measuring her words. "But I do think that would be wise, Parker. We'll get it all under control before somebody gets hurt."

"It's a little odd, don't you think?" Ellie said in a low voice. She and Parker had changed into dry clothes and were sitting on Ellie's woven bedroom rug and leaning their backs against the bed for support. "Mabel and George are unusual, at least when it comes to long-lost relatives, at least as I understand it. But they've been kind to us. And now, all of a sudden, it's like Mabel is *trying* to make you feel guilty for something you didn't do."

She looked at Parker out of the corner of her eye, hoping she hadn't hurt her feelings. Guilt was hard to think around—once Mabel had insinuated that this mounting chaos was Parker's fault, Ellie had felt guilt swelling in her forehead, the back of her neck, her chest—guilt that her own powers weren't strong enough; that she couldn't prove her sister's innocence; that she had for one second thought, *Maybe it's true.*

It was a cold, all-encompassing feeling, and it was hard to step outside of, to clearly see what was going on. Even now, saying it out loud, she wasn't totally sure what was true and what wasn't. What if Parker was causing all the chaos and letting the Danger come close without even realizing it? Or what if Parker was lying to her? She'd hidden the astrolabe stuff after all.

"It just feels off to me," Ellie concluded.

"You do believe me, don't you?"

Ellie waited a beat too long before answering. By the time she opened her mouth, hurt had written itself all over Parker's features, and George was at the door.

"Hello, girls," George said, then paused to cough into his sleeve. He leaned heavily against the doorframe, looking exhausted the way a person does when they're trying to hide it. His eyes were dark and distant, and his face looked as though it would sag several inches if he wasn't straining to maintain a smile. "Sorry to interrupt. Ellie, Mabel said you might like to check on the animals with me."

"Great." Ellie pulled herself to her feet and slipped on the whistle pendant she'd taken to wearing. "Sure you don't want to come, Parker? I'm sure there's plenty of time for you to work on your powers with Mabel afterward."

Her sister shook her head. "I have things to do around here," she said vaguely.

So Ellie followed George downstairs and out to the yard. The sky hadn't yet split open, but it looked ominous, and the clouds were moving faster than clouds should.

"Does it take something from us?" Ellie asked George, as they passed the paddock. "When we use our powers?"

"Using our powers is like using our bodies," George replied. "It can be tiring to use up the amount of energy it takes to heal a barn full of animals. Especially at my age."

Ellie thought about this as they walked. She wondered about exercise. If she exercised her powers, would they grow stronger? If Parker stopped exercising hers, would they become rusty and soft?

They worked in silence, hauling feed to each stall and dressing the animals' wounds. To spare George, Ellie did most of the heavy lifting.

"You're a natural at healing," George told her. "Better than I was at your age."

"Thank you," Ellie said shyly. "Before, in Harborville, I felt like I could feel other people's pain, and animals' too. But being able to take it away—to fix it—is so much better."

George nodded. "Because then you get to let go of it yourself," he said. "Otherwise the weight of it would be too much."

"Is that what's happening to you?" Ellie asked quietly. "Is the weight of everything that's been happening at Haven too much?"

George straightened, placing his water pail on the barn floor. "No, child," he said. "I'm just getting old." He eyed Ellie with new interest. "Would you like to do something different after this?" Ellie nodded. "Come on, then. Wrap up with the feed and we'll explore."

Ellie nodded. She finished in the last two stalls and said goodbye to the animals, giving the wolf a scratch behind its ears.

Thank you, human friend. One day, maybe I can repay you.

"No need," Ellie told it. "You getting better is repayment enough. Just don't eat the other animals on your way out." She winked in order to sound jovial, but actually she meant it.

Ellie followed George out of the barn. They walked in silence, and she absorbed all the sounds she couldn't have heard in Harborville. There was the sound of the trees, a mix of the wind in the branches and the stretchy efforts of the roots of all the plants in the earth. She could hear all the cricks and creaks of green things growing, bending toward the light, unfurling. They were finely tuned instruments, rich in detail and texture. It felt as though George was looking at things he wanted Ellie to see: the sparrows in the trees, the red squirrels dashing across elastic tree branches with reckless abandon. How could a place that had seemed so crusty and asleep when they first arrived suddenly feel so alive?

Around the back of the barn was a snarl of vines and weeds, populated by swarms of gnats. George stopped.

"What do you see?"

"A thicket," Ellie replied. "Or at least something that wants to be." At that, one of the vines snaked toward her across the dirt and clutched her ankle. Ellie shrieked, jumping backward, but the vine was too fast. It wrapped itself around her leg and climbed up her torso before she could react.

"George! What's happening?"

George stood, smiling. "That's a pipe vine," he explained. "A little frisky, isn't it? I think it likes you."

Ellie turned to her, astonished. "But it's—"

"It's showing you it trusts you, and it's responding to your presence," George told her. "After I saw you could heal animals, I suspected your gifts extended even further. You're just as powerful as your sister, Ellie. Together, the two of you . . ." He trailed off. "Well, it's just what we've been needing all this time."

"But George! It's going to choke me!" The vine was wending its way around Ellie's neck. Her heart hammered, and she was growing faint of breath.

"Nonsense," George replied. "You're in control. Tell it to recede."

"Recede!" Ellie shouted. "RECEDE!" The vine continued curling around her, rooting her to the spot with its viselike grip.

"Hmm." George frowned. "I'm afraid this isn't my area of expertise." He moved toward the vine and tried prying it off Ellie, who despite herself was beginning to whimper. George pried and tugged to no avail. The vine, as if it detested Ellie's whimpering, slapped several tendrils over her mouth.

Now Ellie was working herself to a panic.

"Ellie." George's voice was calm, soothing. "You're stronger than this plant. Think of it as you might a pet or a child you're babysitting. It craves discipline. It wants you to give it boundaries."

Ellie took a long breath through her nose. *Her nose.* If the vine covered that too . . .

She concentrated with all her might. She visualized the vine receding, herself taming it with merely a thought. She thought of its pores contracting, its roots curling and shifting beneath the earth, an extension of her hands, her body.

Around her neck and shoulders, the vines loosened. Ellie continued to focus. The vine was her. It was a part of her, just like the way her arms and legs were a part of her. She felt the vine begin to slide off her upper body. She took another deep breath, this time through her mouth. And she funneled all her remaining energy into the vine's release.

When Ellie was done with it, the vine squirmed on the ground like a puppy might in the presence of its owner. And then the blossoms appeared: purple-striped things dripped from it, spreading across the thicket until the entire space was filled with color. When it was done, the vine stilled. Ellie could have sworn she heard it let out a sigh.

"I think I'm ready to go back now, George," she told her uncle.

George stared, stunned. "That was . . ."

"I'm tired," Ellie said. And then she took a step toward George before collapsing in his arms.

"I think we ought not tell Mabel about this," George said carefully, as they made their way back to Haven House thirty minutes later. "Are you feeling any better?"

"Much," Ellie told her. George had brought her water from the animals' supply in the barn and after resting in the shade for a few minutes, Ellie had started feeling like herself again. "But why can't we tell Mabel? That's two things now."

"We'll tell her eventually; I just think we should wait a while," George explained. "Mabel is very anxious about helping Parker learn to command her own powers. Soon we will need to focus on resetting the balance of nature. If she hears about this, she'll have a conniption. I don't want her to worry about your powers too. I can help you with those."

Ellie thought about this as she plodded through the calf-high grass that had grown several inches since she and Parker had arrived. It made sense. But should *she* be concerned about her powers?

"Don't worry," George said, as if he could read Ellie's mind. "You're clearly extremely gifted, Ellie. You were able to control the vine almost immediately; for anyone else, that situation could have been fatal."

"What?!" Ellie exclaimed. "Did you know that when you brought me there?"

"Well, yes. But I had a hunch you were pretty strong." Then George winked. "Ellie! Don't be silly! I did know it was dangerous—but I could have saved you. I didn't step in simply because I wanted you to do the work, not because I couldn't. And see? I was right not to." Then George opened the front door and shepherded her inside.

On her way back to her room, Ellie tiptoed to Parker's door, which was shut tight.

Ellie pressed her finger, silent, on the door. She knocked, then waited. No voice rang out with an invitation to come in. There was no noise at all. Clearly Parker didn't feel listened to, even though Ellie was trying. Ellie remembered staring at Parker's back when Parker had talked to their dad on the phone. How her sister's shoulders had slumped with disappointment. Whatever their father had told Parker that day was locked with her on the other side of that door. Ellie could tell her sister wasn't napping or listening to music with earbuds in. She could sense Parker sensing her. Parker was choosing not to respond, and Ellie had to let her be. She pressed her finger to the door, wishing her sister a sense of peace. Then Ellie retreated down the hall to her own room to tell Arlo and Walter her secret.

CHAPTER SEVENTEEN

The next morning, the sun didn't come out. The day turned from black to gray as smokelike clouds filled the sky and hung over the farm like a bad mood. Hail clattered against Haven's windows, the din so loud it seemed to Parker as if it were seeking her rather than simply ricocheting around. She rolled around in bed, unsuccessfully trying to block out the gloom, but felt too wired to sleep. Her self-control sessions with Mabel had been a disaster. Parker had learned to contain her powers, but inside she was a roiling mess—a bundle of firing nerves and sparking senses threatening to burst forth at any moment. She spent the morning on the covered front porch, watching ice chunks the size of grapes drive holes in the grass that had sprouted around Haven seemingly overnight.

The more Parker controlled herself, the more it seemed her powers grew. And the more she kept them inside her, the worse she felt. Parker had never before thought of her restless energy as bad. She had never thought the way she was could be dangerous . . . until now.

The sky continued to drive icy bullets earthward. They knocked down tree branches, beheaded wildflowers, played ping-pong with the front steps. Parker didn't *feel* like it was all coming from her; she felt as though her own energy was bottled up—something separate from the chaos unfolding around her. But Mabel had assured her that even *having* negative energy was the problem. That Parker was inviting the Danger closer simply by being.

Parker didn't know what to think about this.

At some point, Arlo wandered out of the house and sat next to her. They couldn't communicate the way he and Ellie could, but Parker felt like they were developing a language of their own. Arlo lay down on his belly with his head resting on his paws and glanced at Parker every now and then as if to make sure she was OK.

"You're a nice dog," Parker told him. "I can see why Ellie likes you."

Arlo licked her wrist.

Mabel came down an hour later and bustled around the kitchen, tightlipped. Ellie was still sleeping, and Parker was warming water for the tea kettle. Mabel pulled Mason jars of overnight oats out of the fridge and offered one to Parker. Parker sat opposite Mabel at the big wooden table in the kitchen and listened as the rhythmic sounds of spoons clanking against glass joined the discordant symphony happening outside.

"George probably won't be coming down today," Mabel remarked, scraping her spoon against the sides of her jar to get every last dollop of oats. "He's feeling bad again this morning."

"I wonder if Ellie is feeling bad too," Parker mused aloud. Ellie was often late, but Haven didn't run on a schedule. It was Ellie-like to be scatterbrained about time, but it wasn't like her to sleep late. Next to Parker, Arlo whined.

"Why would Ellie be feeling bad?" Mabel asked sharply. "She's perfectly healthy."

Parker couldn't stand it anymore. "You've been awfully short-tempered lately," she said to her aunt. She set her napkin on the table and her spoon on top of it. "Is there something going on that you haven't told us, Aunt Mabel?"

"No." Mabel shook her head. "Absolutely not. Why would you suggest such a thing? I'm just on edge because I can feel the Danger approaching. I'm worried for you and your sister, and for George."

Parker took a deep breath. She felt as if her insides were being pulled every which way. She thought about all the very good and thoughtful reasons she had given Ellie for not asking about their mother's twin.

Then she chucked them out the window.

"I don't know," Parker said, pretending what she was about to say was just occurring to her. "I've just been thinking about the Danger and wondering where it could be coming from, since I'm pretty sure it isn't me. And then I remembered my mom's best friend."

"Who?" Mabel gave her a strange look. Parker stood casually, collecting their empty dishes and walking them to the sink.

"You know. Sadie. My mom's best friend."

Parker turned back from the sink just in time to see Mabel's fists clench. So. She was onto something, then.

"Or was Sadie my mom's twin?" Parker mused. She knew she sounded calm and collected. On the inside, she was anything but.

"Where did you hear that?" Mabel's voice was ice. Outside, the actual ice was coming down harder. Each piece was nearly golf-ball-size, Parker realized, looking out the window.

"It was just a guess," Parker replied. "All this talk about powers running in our family . . . you and George, me and Ellie. Maintaining balance and working together. It makes sense that my mom would have a twin too. Is it true?"

Mabel hesitated. "It's complicated." She pushed back from the table and wiped her hands on a linen napkin. Her movements looked jagged, as if she weren't quite sure what she should be doing.

"How complicated could it be? Why did you lie to us?" Parker was exasperated. More than that, though, she was afraid.

"*Sadie* was complicated," Mabel said. "We were trying to protect you."

"Why would you need to protect us?"

"Not 'us.' *You,* Parker. We were trying to protect *you.* But you've proven over and over that you don't need to be protected. So, fine. I'll tell you. Just don't expect to like what you hear."

"I can handle it." Parker felt very grown-up just then. She thought about Clara, about her old life of just a week ago, when winning an Ultimate game was the most important thing about her day. So much had happened; so much had changed her since then.

Mabel strode to the sink and pulled open a tiny drawer, which she fished through for a while, scattering paper clips and pencil shavings onto the floor, before retrieving a white envelope and motioning at Parker to join her in the adjacent room.

"Better settle in for this one," Mabel recommended, sitting cross-legged on the floor in front of the fireplace.

"What am I missing?" Ellie was descending the stairs, rubbing her eyes and yawning despite the fact that it was well after ten. She leaned over the bannister, squinting at the two of them.

"Mabel is telling us about Sadie," Parker said quickly, before Mabel could change her mind.

Parker didn't mean to sound smart; it was sort of a thing that happened while her emotions were all bundled up inside. Things just slipped out. The revelation that Mabel and George really *had* been lying to them—that their mom and maybe dad had lied to them too—wasn't helping matters.

"I didn't lie, you know," Mabel remarked, as if she could hear Parker's thoughts. Ellie reached the bottom of the stairs and joined them on the floor of the living room. "Sadie was your mom's best friend. She just happened to also be her identical twin. I left that part out."

"You and George both—" Parker started, just as Ellie said, "It's still a lie."

Ellie looked at Parker. She fidgeted, twirling her whistle necklace on its chain.

Go ahead, Parker tried hard to convey to her through a nod. Ellie seemed to understand.

"Is Sadie dead, then?" Ellie asked. Arlo settled in beside her and rested his head on her thigh.

"She may as well be," Mabel told them. "She disappeared a long time ago. She let the Danger take her. No one knows where she is now."

The hair on the back of Parker's neck pricked. Mabel had danced around the Danger. Parker knew what it was to her—the taunting whispers in the woods, the desire to lose control. Now, finally, she was going to hear more.

"The thing is," Mabel told them, "Sadie killed your mom."

Ellie reacted first.

"*What?*" she shrieked, leaping to her feet.

"Mom isn't dead," Parker said calmly. She had never voiced it aloud before, but there it was.

"Your mother *is* dead," Mabel corrected her, as if she were discussing a roast goose or an unfortunate house mouse. "Ellie, I'll need you to listen, please, if I'm going to continue." Mabel let out a long, irritated sigh and raked her hand through the side of her hair, pulling a few errant strands from her bun. "Perhaps I was a bit dramatic in my delivery. I apologize. What I meant to say is, if Sadie hadn't jumped ship, your mom would likely still be alive. Here."

She opened the envelope, which Parker had forgotten about, and which Mabel had been clutching in her lap.

"Here's the two of them," Mabel said, pulling out a photograph. "That box you found in your mother's room—those were all pictures of Sadie. Ginny was clever, wasn't she? We threw out all those photos after Sadie's betrayal, but Ginny must have collected them from the rubbish bin. We saved one photo of the two of them, because George is a sentimental fool. This is it."

She presented the photo to Parker. Parker stared. It was like looking at two versions of Ellie dressed in throwback clothes. Their arms were wrapped around each other, and the one on the right had her head tilted back in laughter, as the one on the left looked at her fondly, a small smile gracing her features. Parker traced the laughing girl's profile with her index finger.

"That's Sadie," Mabel confirmed.

Ellie scooted closer to Parker and leaned over her shoulder. "Wow," she said. "They look just like me in this photograph." Despite herself, Parker added a jolt of jealousy to the frothing mix inside her.

"They were quite close," Mabel said. "Not like the two of you. Oh"—she chuckled, waving her hand at Ellie's protest—"it's OK, really. Not every set of twins is built to be best friends. I'm sure your uncle George would say I'm an acquired taste."

Parker shifted uncomfortably. It was true that she'd always thought of Clara as her best friend, but that was only because Ellie was something else entirely. Not something less. If anything, she was a piece of Parker, and that was bigger than best friendship. Still, she could see the hurt in her sister's eyes. Ellie had always *wanted* to be closer,

Parker realized. She had tried. Parker had been the one to brush her off as weird, unfit for the sort of friendship Clara offered.

The knowledge made Parker feel awful. She saw Ellie looking at Arlo, who was definitely communicating with his eyes. Parker hoped he was saying something comforting and true.

"Anyway," Mabel went on. "The girls came to Haven just like you two. "When Sadie was a little girl, when her powers were just manifesting, she and your mother were brought here to train in a safe space. They were the same age as you, at the time."

Parker tried to imagine her mother as a young girl, arriving at the farm with Sadie.

"Did she like it here?" Parker asked.

"Your mother loved it here. Like you, Ellie, she immediately developed the power of empathy, the ability to communicate with the natural world. And at the sanctuary that blossomed. She loved the animals and the plants. She loved the sanctuary, although she had bigger dreams: of travel, of seeing other places, helping our planet in more profound ways." Mabel sighed. "Sadie . . ."

Parker felt a knot in her stomach. "Sadie hated it here," she guessed. "She didn't fit in."

"Not exactly," Mabel said. "Everything was OK at first.

Ginny was the stronger one—her powers eventually spanned both animals and the elements. It was the first time we'd ever seen that happen. But Sadie was bright and talented. She could control both wind and rain. Together, they were a force far stronger than anyone who came before them. George and I thought for sure they'd serve nature together, restore harmony to our planet, bring the earth back to a golden age. Fix suffering. Destroy the Danger for good by starving it of victims. It was naïve. The challenge just made the Danger more thirsty, more determined to take the girls' power away.

"For a while, everything was OK. California had never been more temperate. Crops were bountiful, wildfires were rare, and people were at peace. This went on for some time, until they were in their early twenties. Eventually, both girls wanted more. Sadie in particular craved a challenge. The first time they went on a mission together—to combat fires in Texas—well, Sadie got carried away. She liked her power too much, and she was threatened by Ginny's. She forgot to control the dangerous feelings. She overpowered Ginny in a petty moment of showing off and, long story short, a whole lot of people died.

"After that, Sadie started slipping away. She got into trouble, turned inward. She was secretive: snuck out at night, lied to Ginny, lied to us. In the end, we lost her. She ran off with friends one night. Disappeared entirely.

"You have to understand," Mabel continued, "although your mother was the more powerful of the two, Sadie was still quite powerful. From the moment she arrived. She had already been exercising her abilities. Testing her abilities on her own. She wanted to be stronger. Better. From day one, she craved the spotlight."

Mabel turned her head away, "I was so proud of her. So in awe of her ability. I thought of all the things she could do. What good she could do for the planet with her strengths. But."

But.

Parker stared at Mabel. For the first time, her aunt didn't look like a stern person who thought Parker did everything wrong.

"I let her exercise her powers," Mabel said. "I saw her skills improving. But power is never simple," Mabel continued. "Our powers shift and evolve. Our power also comes from somewhere. Long ago, we pulled our strength from the earth. We drew energy from the environment. But that had a price. When we take, we leave a mark. When we take, we take away. When we realized our mistake, our family resolved that we would devote ourselves to helping the natural world, to repair the damage we had done by robbing the earth of its resources.

"You're right that our powers are given to us in pairs," Mabel went on. "We connect with each other, and we draw strength from that connection. That is what makes us strong. But it is not easy. Sadie was wracked with guilt after the disaster in Texas. She could never trust herself again. The more your mother shone, the more she wilted. They couldn't very well maintain balance in nature if they were out of balance themselves."

Parker looked at Ellie, who thought Parker wanted to work with anyone but her.

"How did she kill Mom," Ellie asked quietly.

"Your mom was heartbroken," Sadie said simply. "She met your dad and had you two, and that brought her so much joy. But Sadie's betrayal weakened her. She simply couldn't continue on in the same capacity. Yet she kept pushing herself to solve our planet's problems. She just wasn't strong enough anymore. And so she died doing the work she loved."

"You think I'm like Sadie," Parker realized. "That's why you didn't tell us about her."

Mabel hesitated.

"We saw similarities there," she acknowledged. "We didn't want you to be afraid. George and I didn't want either of you to know what Sadie was capable of. But it also wasn't that calculated. No one's talked about Sadie in years and years, you see. We all stopped talking about her after she vanished. It hurt your mom too much. So when you brought out the photos and the note, we simply didn't know how to react. We knew some day we would need to tell you both everything. We just weren't prepared for it to be *then*. Before you even understood your own powers.

"When your father called the morning of your birthday . . . It was not an easy choice for him, but it was the right choice. He didn't know about your aunt. He wasn't lying to you. He met your mom after Sadie was gone."

Parker thought about Mabel's recent snappishness. Maybe Mabel wasn't short-tempered. Maybe she was scared.

"Your aunt turned her back on her duty to your mom, to this family, to our planet. The Danger got its claws in her, and she gave herself over to it by succumbing to her own pain. Your mother did her best to help us control the impact."

It got its claws in her. Parker recalled the whispers in the woods; the way they'd filled her ears, taunting her, consuming her.

She dropped her head. "I'm not going to be like Sadie," she said firmly.

Mabel knelt next to Parker and placed a hand on her back. "I know you've been frustrated lately. And you're allowed to be frustrated. It's hard knowing you have so much in your hands, so many responsibilities. Anyone would crack under that kind of pressure."

"I don't want to be this powerful," Parker sighed. She felt Ellie studying her. She wondered what it would be like to be Ellie. To have a power that was tame and gentle.

"Well, here we are," Mabel said. "It's a blessing and a curse, isn't it? It's tempting to be like your aunt Sadie. To run away from duty. That would be very easy, wouldn't it?"

To Parker, her words sounded like a challenge. It *would* be easy to go back to her old life in Harborville—to forget this ever happened. To let the world unfurl around her as if she played no part in its fate.

"We aren't running away from any of this. Are we, Parker?"

Parker met her sister's eyes, which were bright and urgent.

"No," Parker agreed. "We're in this together."

CHAPTER EIGHTEEN

After Ellie got dressed, she loaded a tray with tea and toast for George. She carried it all the way up the stairs without spilling a drop and balanced it on one hand while rapping gently on George's door with the other. When George didn't respond, Ellie eased the door open a crack and peeked in. George was sleeping on his side, his rib cage rising up and down methodically. His mouth was open slightly, and he let out great, shuddering breaths. Under the thin fabric of his nightshirt, he looked even more frail and wraithlike than Ellie remembered.

Ellie slipped inside the room and was placing the tray gently on George's bedside table for later, when George's voice—thin and warbly—broke the silence.

"Did you get that from your mother?" George asked. Ellie jumped, and the tray slipped from her fingers and rattled against the nightstand, tea sloshing out the pot's spigot and scalding Ellie's fingertips.

"George! I didn't know you were awake. I'm so sorry."

"Don't be," George said, followed by a wracking cough. "I'm happy to see you, child. Now tell me. That whistle you're wearing is your mother's, isn't it?"

Ellie's hand flew to her chest. "She gave one to me and one to Parker on our birthdays a few years back. How did you know?"

"I remember seeing her with it before she passed," George remarked. "Not too many whistles that look like that. What does it sound like?"

Ellie shook her head, twisting the cold metal between her fingers. "It doesn't. It doesn't sound like anything at all, I mean. It's broken."

George squinted. "Broken? Are you sure? Can I take a look? Here, take a seat." George patted the bedspread next to him, and Ellie sat down. Then she pulled the whistle over her head and handed it to George.

George seemed so old lately. Ellie watched as George ran his wizened fingers over the object, turning it this way and that, peering at it through narrowed eyes.

"Nothing wrong with it," he said, then fell weakly against his pillows.

"There is," Ellie insisted. "It doesn't even work on Arlo. I tried it on our first day. Here, I'll show you." She held the instrument to her lips and blew into it. Nothing. She tried again. Still nothing.

"Curious," George remarked. "Maybe you just don't know what to listen for."

Ellie was getting frustrated with all the intimations about listening. "I'm not sure what you mean," she said stiffly. "It doesn't make a noise at all. There's nothing *to* listen for."

"True. It doesn't make a noise to us. But just because it doesn't work on Arlo or you and me, doesn't mean it's broken," George pointed out. "Maybe we're just misunderstanding its function."

"Hm." Ellie thought about this. "I guess you're right. I thought because it looked like a whistle, it would act like one."

"In my experience, it's always helpful to ask questions rather than assume the simplest explanation is the right one," George explained. His voice sounded hoarser by the second.

"Here," Ellie said, pouring some hot tea into a pretty cup decorated with lilies. "Drink some tea and rest a bit."

George obeyed, accepting the cup. He blew steam off the liquid's surface and took a tentative sip, the cup shaking in his hand. "Peppermint." He let out a satisfied sigh. "My favorite."

"I thought so," Ellie told him. She'd had a feeling.

"Always ask questions, Ellie. Lots of things are more than what they look like."

"That's good advice."

George pressed the whistle back into Ellie's open palm, then folded her fingers over it. "Will you look after the animals today, dear? I'm not sure I have it in me, especially with all that wind. It would blow me right over."

"Sure." Ellie peered out the bedroom window. The hail had stopped falling, thank goodness, but tree branches whipped furiously. She would have to be very careful when she went to the barn. "George, what's wrong?" Ellie asked impulsively. "You fell ill so suddenly, after the hurt animals arrived. I'm worried about you."

"Technically I've been falling ill for eighty-four years."

"I'm being serious," Ellie said. "What's going on?"

George took a wheezing breath. He considered the question.

"I'm not sure," he said finally. "Maybe the healing took it out of me. Maybe I'm simply too old to use my powers that way. I think I'll be OK, though."

"All right," Ellie said. "I'm just worried about you." Then she bent over and gave George a squeeze.

"Just like her," George whispered, his voice muffled where it pressed against Ellie's hair. "Such a caring girl." Then his eyelids fluttered, and he lay his head back on the pillow, exhausted. Ellie picked the tray back up and made her way to the door. George was snoring before she even left the room.

Ellie descended the stairs, thinking about what George had said. She put the whistle to her mouth again with one hand, blowing hard. Still nothing! For all of George's wisdom, maybe it *was* just broken. She was rounding the corner to the kitchen when she encountered Mabel, whose faced was turned down in a grimace.

"Oh!" she said, nearly running right into Ellie's tray.

"Sorry," Ellie said. "I didn't hear you coming. I just got done with George's tea."

"It's all right. How is George?" Mabel massaged her left temple with her thumb. "Does he seem any stronger?"

"Not really," Ellie replied. Her eyes fluttered to the tray, where George's toast sat untouched.

"Oh dear," Mabel said, following Ellie's gaze. "I'll see if I can make a hearty soup later—he may like that. I'm going to go lie down for a bit, Ellie. I have a terrible headache. Keep your sister out of trouble, OK?"

"Parker's fine." Ellie tried not to sound annoyed, but she didn't like how Mabel seemed to think the worst of Parker and seemed to overlook Ellie's powers altogether. "I'm going to ask her to help me feed the animals."

"Terrific," Mabel said, wincing slightly. "I'll see you in soon, then."

An hour or so later, Ellie and Parker—with Arlo in tow, as was always the case now whenever Ellie went somewhere—were feeding and watering the animals and changing the dressings on their wounds, when Ellie heard Parker let out a yelp.

"Ellie! Come quick!"

Ellie dropped her feed pail and ran toward the sound of Parker's voice, fully expecting to see something dire happening to one of the animals.

Instead, there was Parker, looming over two perfectly healthy rabbits and freaking out. She waved her wrist at Ellie. "Do you see this? DO YOU SEE THIS!" she shouted.

"Um. A . . . wrist?"

"NO!" Parker's face was beet red. "It's my bracelet from Mom! It's gone!"

"Oh no," Ellie gasped. Now she understood what all the fuss was about. "It's got to be around here somewhere. "Arlo, go find Parker's bracelet!"

I thought you'd never ask, Arlo commented. He nudged Parker's wrist with his snout, and she let his little twitching nose circle her wrist, taking in her scent. *On it,* he told Ellie, sniffing the ground intently and making a beeline for the barn door.

"He'll find it," Ellie assured Parker. "Don't worry."

"OK, it's just . . ." Parker trailed off, then sat heavily on the floor of the stall. "I think my powers aren't as strong without it."

"Really?" Ellie looked at her curiously. "I've never taken mine off. I wonder if that's true for me too."

"I took mine off to wash up this morning," Parker admitted. "But I could swear I put it back on. Unless I'm remembering incorrectly?"

"Maybe you didn't fasten it right," Ellie suggested. "Either way, though, Arlo will track it down. Seriously. Unless you flushed it down the toilet, he's on it."

Parker groaned. "Don't make me paranoid."

Ellie sank onto the ground next to Parker and started fiddling with her own bracelet. She managed to unhook the delicate latch after two tries and handed it to Parker.

"What are you doing?"

"Hold it for me. I'm going to test your theory."

Ellie stared down at the rabbits.

"Hello," she said aloud. "Can I get you anything? Food? Water?" She waited for their answer. Nothing. "*Hello*," she said again, louder this time. The rabbits looked up at her, and Ellie's relief was tremendous. "Can I do anything for you two," she asked again. Then she focused and listened hard.

Ye—

W—d li—

It was like the radio frequency was off. Like she was trying to tune in and was getting only the static and muted voices beneath it. She had to focus extra hard just to pick up the word "treat."

"Oh my gosh," she said, indignant. "What is *with* animals feeling so entitled to snacks from us? No, you most certainly cannot have a mango. I don't even know where I would get a mango!"

"So it was normal for you." Parker looked crestfallen.

"No," Ellie corrected. "It actually wasn't. I could hardly make out anything. I had to strain really hard to hear the word 'treat.' It makes so much sense that we weren't really aware of our powers until we got our bracelets. Speaking of Mom's gifts, though, George seems to think my broken whistle isn't broken. Can you try it?"

Parker accepted the whistle and put it in her mouth, which wasn't that gross since they were twins and practically had the same saliva. Parker blew on it. Nothing.

"This one might remain a mystery," Ellie acknowledged. She stood up and dusted off her overalls. She accepted her bracelet from Parker and clasped it back onto her wrist.

"Hey, Ellie?" Parker's voice sounded hesitant.

"Yeah?" Ellie's head was elsewhere. In fact, it was filled with a dozen chattering animal voices now that she had her bracelet back on. Ellie sighed. Maybe Parker had had the right idea—even if unintentionally—perhaps a bracelet break was in order.

"Well, since we're talking about Mom's gifts...I have something to tell you. I should have mentioned it earlier. I just wasn't sure what to make of it."

"The astrolabe," Ellie clarified. "I know. I saw it in that weird library room. And I opened your journal. I'm so sorry, Parker! I've been dying to tell you!"

"You read my journal?"

"Only to see if there was a clue about Mom," Ellie said.

"Well, whatever. I figure you'll just read my thoughts straight out of my head now, anyway."

"Ha ha." Ellie rolled her eyes. "Very funny. Really, I'm so sorry. I only read two pages. I saw what you were doing with the astrolabe. First of all, what does it mean? Second of all, you need to tell me how that thing works ASAP because that is so cool."

"Basically, I think Mom left us a map to the years before she disappeared, right up to her last day," Parker said. As she talked, she became more animated. The color was high in her cheeks, a startling contrast against the rest of her pale complexion, and she was waving her hands around as she explained. "You have to use the position of the stars at a given time to figure out Mom's geographical location on that date. It's really cool! Anyway, I have all the locations figured out now except the last one. But Bodega Bay is the second to last!

And that was supposed to be the last place anyone saw her alive. I think she's trying to lead us to her, Ellie."

"Parker . . ."

"I know. You don't believe Mom is alive. But I'm *telling* you, Mom is trying to send us a message. She's out there somewhere. And the coordinates were meant to tell us where."

"Parker, look. I want her with us as much as you do. I really do. But I'm worried about you. What if Mom *is* dead, like everyone thinks? Will you feel let down all over again? Every time you get worked up about Mom, I'm scared you'll be disappointed. And the last coordinate on your list is from five years ago, when Mom died. So how could she be leading us somewhere?"

"You aren't listening to me," Parker said again, her voice low.

"Oh my god," Ellie told her sister. "I really wish everyone would stop saying that. I'm listening to you! I just have like ten animal voices in my head, and all of them are hungry!"

Just then, she heard Arlo barking in the distance. "Do you hear that?"

"Yeah."

"Maybe he found your bracelet! Maybe he hunted down a real live thief!"

"Really?" Parker jumped to her feet, and the two took off in the direction of Arlo's barking. He was outside the house, busily herding someone—Mabel?—up against the house's exterior wall, the one facing the barn.

"What's he doing?" Parker gasped. "Arlo, no!"

"For once, I have no idea," Ellie said grimly, watching the dog hold Mabel in place by nipping at her calves and feet and barking shrilly every time she tried to move.

When the girls reached Mabel and Arlo, Ellie could tell Arlo was agitated.

"Arlo! What's going on?" she said.

"What on earth!" Mabel was shouting. "Get him off me!"

She has it, Arlo told Ellie.

"What?"

Arlo jumped on Mabel, who jerked backward, nearly falling over.

She is wearing the missing bracelet, Arlo said, panting heavily.

Ellie's eyes traveled to Mabel's exposed arms, where she held them aloft to protect herself from the dog. Ellie saw Parker's eyes following hers. Mabel was wearing not one, not two, but *three* bracelets stacked on one wrist. One was Mabel's own. The second was Parker's. But what was the third? Ellie squinted, then let out an involuntary gasp. The third was adorned with tiny stars. It was the bracelet their mom had once worn.

"Mabel, do you have my bracelet on?" Parker asked, incredulous. She hadn't noticed their mom's bracelet. Ellie put a hand on Arlo's back and commanded him to heel.

"Yes!" Mabel was still blocking her face with both her hands even though Arlo had stopped jumping and had settled himself by Ellie's feet. "And for good reason. You're far too dangerous to be wearing your bracelet right now. It'll only make your powers stronger. I saw it lying on the kitchen table and took it for your own good, so you don't hurt yourself. Or us! The last thing we need is you burning the barn down or splitting the house in two. You can have it back once you've mastered your control."

Parker looked as if she'd been slapped.

Liar, Ellie heard Parker say, only to Ellie. *That's not why she took it.* Ellie looked at her sister, and her heart thudded hard behind her ribs. What was Parker implying? Then, *I bet two bracelets makes her doubly strong.* They hadn't discussed it, but Ellie was almost certain she had been able to hear Parker's thoughts recently—at least the ones Parker directed at her.

"Give it to me," Parker said, furious. "It isn't yours."

"I will not," Mabel replied calmly.

Something was very wrong. Ellie needed to speak to someone she trusted. Then she realized: She could call Dad! The house had a landline! And her dad would answer. And he would understand how scary and weird things suddenly were at Haven. And he would have a solution.

While Parker and Mabel argued Ellie bolted for the house, Arlo at her side.

Once inside the house, Ellie spotted the ancient beige plastic phone on its tiny table in the living room. She picked up the receiver and put it to her ear. It was like putting a salad bowl next to your head. She dialed her dad's number and felt a rush of relief when it began to ring.

"Ellie? Parker?"

"Dad?"

"Ellie? Oh thank God you called. I've been trying to get ahold of you all morning."

"You have?"

"I need you to listen to me very carefully, L-Bean, and try not to be scared. You and your sister need to get out of there. I—I think you're in danger. Please. Both of you leave Haven as soon as you can. Go to the train station and buy a ticket, wherever the first train out—"

With that, the phone line went dead.

"Dad?" Ellie shouted into the phone. "DAD?"

"What did he say?"

Ellie looked up. Parker was standing next to her, her wrist still bare. Ellie hadn't even heard her come in. She was staring at Ellie, wide-eyed. She looked afraid.

Mabel was standing next to her. Leveling Ellie with her glare.

"I need to call my dad back," Ellie said, holding out the receiver. Her hand was shaking. She tried to steady it, but that just made it worse. "I thought this phone worked."

"It does," Mabel said, pulling off her work gloves.

"It's broken," Ellie tried not to sound hysterical, but her whole body was vibrating. She hit the power button, then hit it again. Nothing.

"It's the phone lines," Mabel explained. "Sometimes they go out. Especially with a storm. What do you need that's so urgent, Ellie? I'm sure your dad can wait till the power's back, can't he?"

Ellie placed the phone back in its stand and nodded slowly. *Wait till the power is back.* It was funny. Ellie wanted to laugh. *The power is everywhere,* she wanted to shout. *Everywhere except this stupid phone!*

She wanted to tell Mabel what her dad had said. But something in her resisted. She needed to talk to Parker first. She stared at Parker, trying to signal her with her eyes. But Parker wasn't paying attention.

Mabel was though.

"Come now," Mabel said, putting a hand on Ellie's shoulder and steering her away from the phone. "It's not as bad as all that. Here." She fished in her overall bib for a fresh handkerchief and handed it to Ellie. Now Parker was focused on Ellie. She was giving her a look of concern.

Ellie thought about what George had told her earlier, about how things weren't always what they looked like on first glance.

Mabel's eyes were narrowed, and she gave her cheek a light tap with one finger.

Ellie reached up to touch the same spot on her own face, and her hand came back damp.

It was only then that she realized she'd been crying.

PART III:

HAVEN'S SECRET

CHAPTER NINETEEN

"**W**hat's all this?"

George had materialized at the bottom of the staircase. He wore a long raincoat over his pajamas and carried a wallet.

"The phone isn't working," Mabel explained. "And Ellie is upset."

"Oh well, I'm sure it'll be working soon. Mabel is very good with electronics. Isn't that right, Mabel?" George asked. "A real whiz."

"Of course. You've just got to be patient, Ellie."

Parker looked at her sister, whose face projected conflicting feelings. It was all there, written on her features for everyone to see: frustration, anger, worry, *fear*. Parker didn't know what their dad had said to Ellie on the phone, but Ellie seemed rattled.

Parker was used to being the turbulent one. Now that Ellie was unsteady, she was experiencing something unfamiliar: an eerie calm, like a weighted blanket settling onto her chest and limbs. It was almost as if together, they were a teeter-totter that had reversed positions. Someone always had to be OK, didn't they? Or they would fly off their axis the way Sadie had, and their mom in turn. Arlo gave Ellie's hand a nibble, and she scratched his head. The exchange of affection seemed to calm her.

"Why are *you* out of bed?" Mabel asked George. "Come now. Are you feverish? You're not thinking of going out there, are you? Let me help you out of that," Mabel said, reaching for her twin's raincoat.

"I thought I'd go to town," George informed them, side-stepping Mabel with no shortage of effort. "I need my lozenges and we seem to be out." He swayed on his feet, gripping the bannister hard with one hand.

"Well," Mabel stuck her hands in her pockets. She seemed to be waging an internal battle. "I don't want you to be without lozenges, but you certainly can't drive."

"I need them," George said again. "My throat is intolerable. Debating the issue is only making it worse."

"My library book is due back," Ellie suddenly said from the corner of the living room. Parker glanced in her direction and noticed Arlo, who winked—not at her, but at George. *He winked!* What was more, George winked back, out of Mabel's field of vision. Parker was beginning to catch on to what was happening.

Mabel threw up her hands in frustration. "Fine!" she said. "But someone needs to stay with George, and I want to keep an eye on you, Parker. Ellie, you can give Parker your library book to return. I'll get George's lozenges while you do it. We won't be long."

What did Dad say? Parker thought urgently in the direction of her sister. Ellie just ran up the stairs, though, and returned a second later with a romance novel with a big pink curly title and a girl in a fancy dress on the cover, which she pressed into Parker's hands. *Really?* Parker thought.

"Don't judge," Ellie said with a haughty air. Then she spun on her heel and helped George back up the stairs. It was hard to tell whether she'd actually heard Parker or just *knew* Parker.

The second they pulled up in front of the blue Victorian library-house, Parker sprang out of the car.

"I'll be back in ten minutes," Mabel called after her. "Be waiting in front of the building when I arrive." Parker ignored her, dashing up the library steps instead. She'd try to email their dad on the ancient desktop if she could.

The library was completely deserted except for the librarian, who was leaning on the front desk wearing an elaborate green-velvet pantsuit and bright blue rhinestone glasses. Her hair was piled up on her head and tied with a green scarf. There was a bedazzled sign on the desk that read Ms. Boudin in rainbow stones contrasted against fake diamonds.

Clearly Ms. Boudin was game to talk about accessories. She was wearing all of them.

"Well, that was fast," Boudin waved, her fingernails covered in a bright purple polish. "Ellie's already done?"

"Yeah, well," Parker held up the book and placed it on the desk. "She probably wanted to avoid late fees. I'm just here for the Internet."

Boudin stood up straight and evaluated Parker. "Very farm couture," she said, taking in Parker's overalls.

"Oh!" Parker blushed, embarrassed. She'd forgotten what it was like to get dressed like a person who didn't live at Haven. "It's just so I don't get dust on my regular clothes."

"Sure." Boudin pushed a new Polly Marker book toward Parker. "For your sister," she explained. "It just came in."

Polly Marker books were all about girls going on extravagant worldwide vacations to places like Amsterdam and Rome and London, all with many color-coordinated suitcases and handbags. Inevitably, each protagonist fell in love at the Colosseum or whatnot. Ellie was so weird. Parker preferred graphic novels about girls who toured worldwide with professional sports leagues.

"Paris, huh?" Parker said, picking up the book. "Glamorous. Ellie will love this."

"Certainly more glamorous than around here." Boudin sighed, tapping her hair comb with a manicured finger. "This place is about as glamorous as the bottom of a boot."

"Not a lot of overalls and big old rubber boots in Paris," Parker grinned.

"None," Boudin smiled back. "Also, way fewer cows."

"And people who talk to cows," Parker quipped.

Boudin burst into a cackle so loud it startled Parker, who felt a pang of guilt. That was a total secret! Why had she said it? Furthermore, she only had about five minutes left and *had* to email her dad.

That was why George had winked at Arlo, wasn't it? Because they had orchestrated this whole thing? Because he knew Ellie and Parker wanted to talk to their dad?

When she thought about it that way, it sounded kind of ridiculous.

"I'm in kind of a rush," Parker said. "My aunt's coming back in a few minutes, and I really need to use the computer. Are we good here?" She hadn't meant to sound rude—just informative—but Boudin's smile faded.

"Of course," she said. "Let me just check you out." She pulled out a rubber stamp and flipped it to the correct date. It seemed to take forever. Parker shifted from side to side. Boudin opened the book to the front cover.

"Oh!" she said, sounding surprised. "I'm sure this writing wasn't here when I lent this book to Ellie. I'm afraid I'll have to issue you a fine."

"What?" Parker leaned over the desk, impatient. "What fine? What writing?"

Ms. Boudin peered at Parker over the top of her glasses and slid the book toward her. "See for yourself."

Parker flipped it open and stared.

The book was definitely defaced.

And the writing was definitely Ellie's—big, bold, capital letters read:

DAD SAYS SOMEONE IS AFTER US

Subtle. "Well." Parker slapped the book shut and tucked it under her arm. "I should go," she said. "You can charge that to our aunt's account."

"Your aunt doesn't have an account," Boudin told her. "I'm going to have to insist you leave that here," she told Parker. "I'll waive the fee this time since it's a first offense and it's in pencil, which I can erase. But here, let me sort this new book out."

"Oh, don't bother," Parker replied, handing over the book. She didn't even care about the computer anymore. What if

Boudin was after them? This lady had been overly friendly from the very first second they'd met. At the time, Parker had been distracted by the promise of the Internet and had dismissed it as desperation. After all, what kind of middle-aged lady befriended young girls? A suspicious one, for sure. At the time, Parker had thought "a lonely and bored one." But now she knew better. Sinister vibes were rolling off Ms. Boudin in waves as pungent as Arlo's toots after too many table scraps.

"I'm just going to go," she said as Ms. Boudin stamped the new book and began jotting something on the inside. "Really. Ellie can come back some other time."

"I'll just be a minute," Ms. Boudin said. "Have you ever lived anywhere else?" She ignored Parker's obvious efforts to leave.

"Oh—oh," Parker stammered— it was obviously rude to ignore someone's question. And what if Ms. Boudin was trying to be friendly? Maybe she wasn't sinister. Maybe she was just awkward. She was a librarian after all. Parker wouldn't want to be rude if that were the case. It was all extremely confusing.

"Um. Harborville. You?" Parker's thoughts were all jumbled up. Was Ms. Boudin nice or not nice? Why was Mabel so mean? What had Dad said to Ellie about someone being after them? Who was after them?

Dad. The entire reason Parker and presumably Ellie and maybe even George had finagled this trip to town.

"I've lived lots of places," Boudin said, pulling a magazine from under her desk. "All over the world. Now I'm stuck here. Like you."

"I've *got* to use the Internet," Parker said loudly. "Right now."

"Well then." She put down her pencil and pushed the book in Parker's direction. "I've finished checking you out. Just sign the card and let's go."

Parker retrieved the pencil and opened the new book, signing on the library card that was tucked into an envelope pasted to the inside front.

"You didn't even read it," Boudin said, looking miffed. "I took time to write the return date down for you. "I went the extra mile."

"I'll look later." Parker was growing desperate. She pulled out her iPhone and looked at the time—if Mabel was prompt, Parker had three minutes left. "Can you *please* log me on to the computer now?"

"Yes, but I suggest you lower your voice. This is a library after all." Parker looked around her. They were the only ones in the building as far as she could tell.

Boudin began walking briskly down the hall toward the room where the ancient computer was kept. Now Parker practically had to skip to keep up.

"Where would you go?" Boudin asked as they strode into the room and Parker dashed over to the computer. Boudin hovered over the table and took her time logging on, as if they hadn't a care in the world. She adjusted her glittery glasses. "If you could go anywhere."

"I don't know," Parker said absently. "I really just wanted to get home to Harborville and school and my friends a couple days ago, but a lot has changed since then." The little wheel was spinning. Parker tap-tap-tapped her fingers on the table. It was taking *forever*.

Boudin pulled up a chair next to Parker and plopped into it. Parker stared at her, surprised. For the first time, Ms. Boudin gave Parker a very serious look. Parker could almost see her eyes boring through the thick glass of her spectacles.

"Listen," she said. "Don't you get stuck here if it's not where you want to be. You hear me? Trust your gut. If you have any way of leaving, leave. Before it's too late and you *can't* leave. Maybe you should leave today."

"Why wouldn't I be able to leave?" Parker watched the wheel turn, distracted.

Boudin hesitated. "No reason," she said brightly. "I'm just here to look after you. Because that's what librarians do. By the way, I slipped the train schedule into that Polly Marker book. Just in case."

"Uh-huh." Parker was opening her email. Waiting, waiting.

Finally, it logged her on.

Still nothing from Clara. But Parker didn't have time to dwell on it. She opened a new message and dashed off a note to her dad. She told him exactly how to get to Haven. *I DON'T KNOW WHAT'S GOING ON, BUT SOMETHING'S NOT RIGHT*, she typed. *PLEASE COME.* Then she hit send, feeling relieved. She'd done it.

The wheel spun.

And spun.

And spun.

"What is *with* this dumb machine!" Parker slammed her palms on the table in frustration just as a horn sounded outside. "Shoot, shoot, shoot! I told her I'd meet her out front." Parker heard a car door slam shut. She imagined how angry Mabel would be that she was screwing up once again. "Ahhh," she groaned. "I have to go."

"I'll make sure it sends," Boudin assured her.

Boudin was surprisingly helpful about computer matters, despite how clueless she seemed otherwise.

"OK! OK. Thanks," Parker told her, shooting out of the chair.

"Don't forget Ellie's book," Boudin called, handing the discarded Polly Marker book to Parker.

"Right." Parker run-walked out of the room.

"And don't forget to look at the due date in the front!" Boudin called after her. "You're welcome!"

Mabel was just striding into the entrance when Parker whizzed out, nearly smacking right into her. Parker instinctively slipped the Polly Marker novel under her windbreaker. She didn't know what had compelled her to hide it; it just happened.

"Sorry, Mabel!" Parker said. "That took forever. Did you get the lozenges? Let's get a move on."

Mabel gave her a once-over then nodded, turning back toward the truck. "I'm not in a real parking spot," she grumbled. "I didn't realize I would *have* to park."

"Sorry," Parker said again.

Ellie's written message seemed to stick on her mind the whole way home. Which was why—when they drove through Main Street and she spotted two teenagers from behind (dark-haired and decked out in identical watermelon-patterned outfits and knee-high galoshes)—she stiffened. Those teens, who were placing an order at the ice-cream stand, looked suspiciously like the hoodie-and-umbrella teens, who had looked a lot like the Phillips twins from Harborville Upper School. It was weird. Very weird. It wasn't as if Bearsted was a hopping tourist destination. But why would Casey and Cassie Phillips be following them? What could they want from her and Ellie? Why had Boudin been acting so strangely?

Parker shuddered. The only thing she knew was, they needed to get out of Bearsted *STAT*. And there was no way they were going to do that under Mabel's eagle eye.

They rode over a pothole and the truck jounced, making the book dig painfully into Parker's waist. She pulled it out from under her jacket, glancing at Mabel in the rearview mirror. Mabel had her eyes on the road.

Parker opened the book, and the train schedule dropped out onto her lap. Boudin hadn't been kidding then. Well, maybe it would be helpful. It was weird, though, how much Boudin seemed to want Parker to get out of town. Parker flipped to the front cover. Boudin had yammered on about dates, but Parker didn't even see a date there! Instead there was a long reference number under a signature line, followed by *Branch Location: Haven*. Huh. The library was located in Bearsted. Haven was just the name of the sanctuary. Why had she written "Haven"?

There was something else that didn't make sense. Parker peered closer. Why did the reference number look so familiar?

"Oh no," she whispered, though not quietly enough. She looked up to find Mabel's eyes on her own in the mirror. Parker tucked the book back under her jacket as carefully as she could, trying not to move. *No, no, no,* she thought deep inside.

"Something the matter?" Mabel asked. Ellie shook her head and forced a smile.

But something *was* the matter. There was very much something the matter.

Because Parker suddenly remembered why the book's reference number looked so familiar.

It wasn't a reference number at all.

Unless you counted astrolabe coordinates as a reference number.

And if you did, the reference number would be *Branch location: Haven.*

Haven.

The very last place their mother was seen alive.

CHAPTER TWENTY

Ellie was midconversation with Arlo when Parker spilled in, nearly breaking down the door. She was very obviously clutching something under her jacket and very obviously motioning to Ellie with her chin (by very obviously jutting it toward the second-floor bedrooms) and very obviously scream-talking at Ellie:

CAN YOU HEAR ME BECAUSE THERE IS SOMETHING WE NEED TO DISCUSS

"George's been asking for you," Ellie told Mabel, who stood behind Parker, looking peeved.

"Oh?" Mabel sounded doubtful.

"Yes. He said to tell you to bring the lozenges because he has to tell you something." Ellie held her breath. It was a total lie and Ellie wasn't used to lying, so it was the best she could come up with on the fly. Mabel gave her a skeptical look, then shrugged.

"OK. I'll be back in a minute." She slid out of her jacket and draped it over a hook that had been fashioned from a taxidermy deer hoof, which Ellie had somehow overlooked till now. She recoiled.

"No way did George OK that," she commented after Mabel hastened up the stairs, lozenges in hand.

"Ellie! We have *way bigger problems,*" Parker exclaimed.

"What? I know. Did you email Dad? Did you get my note?"

"Yes!" Parker whisper-shouted, pushing Ellie out of view of the stairs. "And look at this!" She shoved the book into Ellie's hands.

"Oooh!" Ellie exclaimed, temporarily forgetting their circumstances. "The new one! How does she do it?" Boudin was a book hero.

"Argh! Ellie, that is not the point. Open to the title page. Hurry!" Parker glanced toward the stairs, aware that Mabel could return at any second. Ellie did as she was told. She squinted at the coordinates, confused. "What is this?"

"It's *Haven,*" Parker said, obviously exasperated. "The last coordinates on Mom's list! Boudin made this big, weird deal out of suggesting I get away, then she tucked *a train schedule* inside the book, then she wrote down these numbers, and I couldn't figure out why they looked so familiar, but they're Mom's last coordinates that I couldn't figure out! Don't you get it? *Branch location: Haven.* The coordinates point to Haven!"

"I don't . . . but . . . what does it *mean*?"

"It means Mom was here the day she disappeared," Parker

said, keeping her voice low. "It means maybe someone here was responsible for Mom's disappearance. Someone like *Mabel*."

Ellie sucked in a breath. On the one hand, Parker was going on about her conspiracy theories again and Ellie didn't want to encourage her. On the other . . .

"Mabel was right next to me when I was calling Dad," she said. "Parker, why is there no power in the house at all, except when we need it? Why is there *only* electricity when it comes to the landline? But we use lanterns and candles for bed, and somehow they're always lit at the right time, and somehow every time we've gone exploring, the corridors are always lit?" She couldn't believe they hadn't thought of it before.

"Because Mabel controls it." Parker's voice was urgent. "She's the one controlling it."

"Which means she has more powers than just hurricane-level wind control," Ellie deduced.

"Which means she purposefully cut the power off when you were talking to Dad," Parker said.

"Which means she might possibly have even more powers we don't know about. Which also means *she* might have been the one causing the weather issues she said *you* caused," Ellie concluded.

The girls looked at each other. Ellie thought of Mabel's headaches.

It sounds like you two have everything figured out, a voice boomed in Ellie's head. She clapped her hands over her ears. *Oh, child. You'll never stop hearing me now.*

"What? What is it, Ellie?"

Ellie sank to the ground, clasping her hands over her ears as Mabel's hideous, booming laughter sounded inside her head. Arlo barked and turned circles beside her, working himself to a frenzy.

"Ellie! Tell me!" Parker sounded hysterical.

Then Ellie looked up from her crouched position to see Mabel hurtling down the stairs toward them.

The whistle, Arlo suggested, just behind the din of Mabel's shrieks. *Use it.*

Ellie reached to her chest. She lifted the whistle to her lips. And she blew into it with all her might.

Mabel clutched her own ears now, keening. She sank to her knees on the stairs, sliding down several steps before coming to a rest on her side. Ellie blew the whistle long and hard, and Mabel screeched as if the pain of the entire world was upon her.

Parker reached out to Ellie, cradling her in her arms. From the center of the living room, they could see Mabel writhing in pain. Their mother had given them the whistle for protection, Ellie realized. She wondered if Mom knew it would be protection against their own aunt. But *why* had Mabel come after them? And what had happened to their mom? Ellie withdrew the whistle, and Mabel sank to the ground.

"What are you doing?" Parker whispered. "She'll come after us!"

"We need answers," Ellie said. "And we won't get them this way. Not by hurting her."

Mabel lay motionless on the stairs, but the room was turning cold around them. Ellie turned to Parker. They should run. They should get out of there—she knew it. But something was holding her back.

"The compass," she said.

"What?"

"Mom's compass. It's in my room. We can't leave without it."

"Ellie, be serious." Parker's eyes were wide. "Mabel is *on the stairs*. We have to leave before she wakes up. We can't get the compass. It's too dangerous."

"It's too dangerous to leave it," Ellie told her. She knew she was right; she could feel it. "Every single thing Mom gave us has been important so far," she reminded Parker. "Everything we thought was broken has worked. So let's get the compass and run out of here."

"What about George?" Parker said.

"I don't know," Ellie admitted. "Is George after us too? I don't know, Parker. I don't know why this is all happening. I just know we need to leave. We can get answers later."

Parker took a deep breath. "OK," she said finally. "Let's go get the compass. But then we're out of here."

I'll go see if she's awake, Arlo offered. *I'll be able to tell if she's faking or not.*

That possibility hadn't occurred to Ellie.

"OK," she said. "Thanks, Arlo. He's going to make sure it's safe," she explained to Parker.

Arlo ambled over to Mabel, who was sprawled across three separate stairs. He got his nose very close to hers and sniffed all along her face. Mabel didn't stir.

She's out for now, Arlo said.

Ellie took a cautious step forward and Parker did the same. Emboldened, she stepped over Mabel's body, heaving a sigh of relief when she was a couple of stairs above. Then Ellie stopped abruptly. She heard something—another voice, faint. Not Parker's, not Arlo's, not even Walter's. She paused, listening hard.

"What are you doing?" Parker whispered. "Hurry up!"

Ellie shook her head. "Shh." She listened as hard as she good. The voice became clearer. More familiar. Words and phrases emerged one by one, until they formed phrases, sentences, a plea.

"Parker," Ellie said, her heart thrumming. "I hear Dad."

"What? What do you mean?"

Ellie fought to stay calm. "He's in danger," she told her. "He's calling to me. He's trying to get to us. He's asking for help. He's somewhere nearby, or I wouldn't be able to hear him."

"No." Parker's face paled.

Ellie struggled to stay calm. "I have to go find him," she said. "Arlo. Can you help me find Dad?"

Yes, Arlo said. *I can sniff him out.*

"Go," Parker said. "He needs you. I'll get the compass. I'll meet you in town at the train station."

"Will you be OK?" Ellie pushed back her panic, struggled against the tears she desperately wanted to shed.

"I'll be fine," Parker told her. "Now hurry! Listen for me, OK? I'll try to tell you when I'm on my way."

"OK."

Mabel shifted on the stairs, groaning a bit. Her eyelids fluttered. Ellie and Parker exchanged terrified glances.

"Go," Parker repeated.

Ellie and Arlo turned back, stepping carefully over Mabel, who let out a grunt when Arlo's paw brushed her thigh.

And then they were off, bounding toward the sound of her father's frightened voice.

Parker scrambled up the rest of the stairs and ran to Ellie's room. She knew exactly where the compass was because what

Ellie didn't know was that Parker had returned several times when Ellie was out caring for the wounded animals, to look at the photos that she now knew were of Sadie and not Mom. The compass was in the nightstand drawer next to these photos. Parker had seen it and disregarded it time and again.

Now, staring down at the brass instrument cradled in the palm of her right hand, Parker was certain Ellie had been right. The compass had a purpose. Maybe, just maybe, it would lead them to their mom. Parker slipped it in her pocket and was about to scramble back down the stairs when she caught sight of Walter, Ellie's dumb fish, swimming from side to side at the front of his bowl, looking agitated.

Parker groaned. She turned, moving toward the door.

Ughhh, she thought to herself. Then, in Ellie's direction: *I hope you know I might die trying to save your stupid fish!*

But what could she put him in? She couldn't run with a bowl!

Then she remembered the teapot George had been using the past couple of days. It had a nice, secure lid, and a spout that would let air in. It would work. George hadn't made a peep this entire time. He was probably sound asleep or passed out from the cold medicine.

Parker gathered Walter's bowl in her arms and tiptoed into George's room. She saw the teapot first. "Yes!" she whispered. She hadn't been certain it would be there still.

She saw George second. George was seated upright, wide awake. Parker froze.

"There are a few things we need to discuss before you run off," George said.

"Where are we going?" Ellie called to Arlo as they ran down the country road away from Haven. The stone wall was behind them now, and the road's packed gravel kicked up little clouds with each heavy step. Ellie had no desire to share Parker's powers, but some of her sister's three-sports-a-year endurance would come in handy right about now. "Where's Dad?"

I am sensing Danger and a human who smells like you, Arlo said, panting heavily (though less heavily than Ellie, being accustomed as he was to long days of herding and sprinting and nipping at heels). *On the train tracks.*

The tracks. Ellie thought back to her train ride to Bearsted. The route had been beautiful—it was as if they threaded impossible pathways in midair as they wended their way through the mountains and across riverbeds, spanning steel bridges that carved arches into the canyons between sheer cliffs.

"Is he close?" she asked Arlo.

Yes. I couldn't smell him otherwise, and you couldn't hear him otherwise.

It took them a half hour to reach the ramshackle train station. By the time they got there, Ellie was sweating buckets and her vision was exploding with little white starbursts. She bent over with her hands on her knees, fighting to catch her breath in the deep shadows of the station's gabled roof.

"Where is he, Arlo? There's no train here." Hoping this wasn't simply the first stop on a marathon journey, she vowed that she would run till her lungs burst if that were what it took—she just hoped she could reach her father before that happened.

There.

The dog was gazing southward, snout thrust forward and ears pointed toward the steep cliffs that faced the river. Ellie followed Arlo's eyes, which were fixed on something in the distance.

"Oh no," Ellie gasped. "Arlo, no."

There, perhaps a half mile from where they stood, was a train.

This train wasn't moving. It wasn't doing anything a train should be doing.

This train was tilted, half suspended in the air over the side of a jagged, mountainous ledge, as if held in the palm of some giant's craggy hand. Far below, a large crater marked the absence of earth beneath one of the beautiful old suspension bridges, now collapsing inward from lack of support. From the teetering train to the lunar hole in the ground, the magnitude of the destruction left her stunned. It was as if she was standing at the edge of a hurricane or walking among the aftermath of a tsunami. Things on this earth—*most* things—were far bigger than Parker, Ellie, Haven. What she witnessed now was no accident—it was the result of power taken to an extreme conclusion. It was Mabel's doing; Ellie felt the truth and horror of it deep inside. Is this how it all would end, every time? Who could be trusted to wield such force?

Ellie? Parker?

There was a time, Ellie knew, when George and Mabel had trusted each other completely.

"Arlo, go find Parker and bring her back here," Ellie said. "I'm going to need her help."

As the dog ran back toward Haven, Ellie ran along the tracks toward the train. As she approached, voices filled her ears.

Panicked voices, scared voices, voices praying to God for the first time or the millionth time, all thinking it will be the last time. Children crying. Beneath it all, her father. *You can do this, Ellie,* he thought at her. *You can make this right.*

Ellie ran toward the train as swiftly as her burning legs could carry her.

Parker froze.

"There are a few things we need to discuss before you run off," George said.

"I don't know what you mean," Parker lied.

"You can trust me, Parker," George told her, coughing a bit into a handkerchief. "I'm not out to get you. Mabel is, apparently. But I didn't know that until today."

"Why should I believe you?" Parker asked, her hands clenched into fists at her sides.

"Because I'm dying," George said simply. "I have nothing to lose."

Parker let out a choked sob. It was all too much. She *liked* George. She didn't want George to die. And yet, through her grief, mistrust swirled. What if this was simply another layer of deception? How could she know?

"Listen closely," George said, keeping his voice low. "Look at me, and focus through your tears. You're strong, Parker. We only have a few minutes. But there are things you need to know."

Parker nodded. "OK," she said, focusing on George's words, forcing herself to stay on high alert. If this were some kind of trap, she would be ready for whatever George and Mabel unleashed next.

"First of all," George said, "Mabel is trying to kill me." Her uncle paused. Parker thought he might be catching his breath, but then she saw tears moisten the corners of George's eyes. "My own sister." His voice had dropped to nearly a whisper. "My twin. I wasn't sure at first, but now there's no doubt in my mind. We're connected, she and I, no matter how hard she tries to disguise what she's really up to. I can feel it. I always could, perhaps I just didn't want to admit it to myself. She's absorbing as much of my power as she can, and probably yours too—and for that I am truly sorry."

"George—" Parker wanted to say how sorry *she* was, how much she hated that this was happening; how if she were George's sister, nothing in a million years would make her betray him. But George held up a hand, silencing her.

"When all's said and done, I think we'll find that you're young enough to withstand it. I'm not. So our time is growing short. You need to know that the powers don't just run in *our* family. This is bigger than just us. Lots of other people have powers. Everyone who has them is a twin of a twin—a twin with at least one parent who's a twin. Most people with powers operate from a home base—ours is Haven. We protect our little part of the planet. When something catastrophic in scale happens, we are sometimes asked to support other branches in other parts of the country. Your mom was called to do that often at first, due to the strength of her powers."

"Branch location: Haven," Parker murmured. It felt good to let her mistrust melt away. George was letting her in.

"Yes, that's right. There are others like us, all working to ward off the Danger. Or at least, that is the hope. It seems my own sister has lost focus. She has fought to keep me weak in order to become more powerful herself.

"You and Ellie are powerful. So powerful. Ellie doesn't even realize the extent of her abilities because she is so used to being overlooked. No," George said, when Parker flushed. "It's not your fault. But do not underestimate your sister. I thought, when you first arrived, that Mabel had good intentions; please believe me. But I know now that she's been trying to keep Ellie's abilities from flourishing, and she is trying to prevent you from exploring your own. Worst of all, she's been trying to turn you two against one another. It appears she wants to take things into her own hands. And when I began to suspect it a few days ago . . . that's when she started taking my power. I could no longer serve her agenda. I knew too much."

"Oh, George." Parker nearly wept. She moved toward her uncle and kissed his wrinkled cheek.

"Don't worry, sweetheart. I will do what I can to take care of myself." The stairs creaked. George's eyes widened.

"Hurry, get your sister's fish. You must go." Parker nodded. Fighting to keep her hands steady, she poured the fish and its water into the empty teapot. "The last thing, though," George continued, "is that I think Mabel may have—"

"May have what, George?"

Parker whipped around, sloshing some of Walter's water out of the kettle's spigot.

"No," she whispered. "No, no, no." Mabel was standing ramrod straight in the doorway, and her eyes were glowing a dazzling blue. Showers of sparks danced from her irises and arced down to the floor trailing thin ribbons of black smoke. If Parker hadn't known better, she would have thought it was beautiful. She stood, transfixed, as the black smoke curled and twined into patterns that slithered toward the corners of the room, seeking cracks in the floorboards.

"Run, Parker," George commanded. "I'll take care of it."

So Parker did—or at least she tried—clutching Walter to her chest as the air grew frigid around them. An arctic wind kicked up. It clawed at Parker's hair and thrust its icy hands into her face and arms, preventing her from moving forward. She pushed through it, willing it back, while George used what Parker knew must be the last of his energy to call in a favor.

The house began to tremble and quake. A noise like a deep foghorn rumbled beneath Parker's feet. The window in George's room burst inward. Glass shards skittered across the floor. Parker focused on the rain outside the window, drawing it into her own private tempest, thrusting it against Mabel's wintry hailstorm. The two storms crashed together above George's bed, and he lifted a frail arm to shield his face from the deluge of rain and hail.

Parker gathered her strength and *pushed*. At first it was like leaning against a brick wall to try to shove it forward. She tasted blood in her mouth. Her vision swam.

"Stay strong, Parker," George shouted from behind her.

Parker was strong. But she needed help, and Ellie wasn't there to give it to her.

She felt weak, incapable of battling the incredible force of Mabel for much longer. All she could do was maintain their stalemate and wait until Mabel's lifetime of practice wielding her power triumphed.

Delaying the inevitable.

At the same time, the roof shrieked as it began to peel off of Haven's walls like the lid on a tin of beans. A crack raced across the floor of the bedroom. Smoke poured from the fresh scar in the gorgeous old planks.

"You're destroying Haven!" Parker shouted. Surely, despite everything Mabel had done, she would have some small shred of love remaining for her home?

"All things are returned to the earth sooner or later, Parker," Mabel said. "In this case—sooner."

The hailstorm battered away at Parker's tempest. Mabel seemed to have boundless energy. A collection of feathers ripped from its moorings on a high shelf and disintegrated in the assault. Parker heard George cry out from his bed, his voice nearly swallowed up by the battling storms. Mabel scrunched up her face and seemed to refocus her energy. The trembling house was a symphony of sudden wreckage—shattering ceramics, twisting metal, a thousand little knick-knacks turned to dust. A busted ukulele with strings like frayed wires went zipping past Parker's face.

Somewhere, cats began to hiss and yowl. A music box raced madly toward the end of its cheery song, then went silent. A hole opened beneath George's bed, and one corner collapsed as the bed listed like a raft in a stormy sea.

Just as Parker was on the brink of despair, a snarl came from the hallway. Parker saw two red pinpricks—eyes!—just behind Mabel. It growled. Startled, Mabel's hailstorm faltered, its assault on Parker's exposed arms and face weakening.

That's when the wolf Ellie had healed chose its moment to spring onto Mabel's back.

Mabel shrieked. Great chunks of ice fell to the floor. Pressure released.

For a second, everything was calm—the eye of the hurricane. Parker took the opportunity to run past Mabel and the wolf. In her peripheral vision, a blur of crimson, a flash of claws and teeth—and then Parker was gone, out of George's room, down the stairs.

The foghorn bellowed from someplace deep inside the house. The sound of the house itself crying out, Haven's last gasp. A metal hubcap ripped from the ceiling and flew past Parker's face, nearly hitting her. Pieces of the tin ceiling ripped free and shot through the air like darts. Parker had just made it out the door with Walter when the entire house let out a long shriek, the sort of noise that betrays pure agony. Mabel's assault might have been interrupted, but the damage had been done.

Haven House split in two, spewing its parts across the land.

Parker ducked, cradling the teapot to her chest with one hand and shielding her head with the other. Pieces of all the lives lived at Haven rained down around her, leaving steaming pockmarks in the lawn. Finally the wind stopped howling and the house stopped moaning, and all was quiet. Parker lifted her head and looked around her. Parts of Haven, carefully constructed by generations of Power siblings, were everywhere.

Oh, George.

She started to scan the wreckage for George's bed, but hardly had time to think about it before three sharp barks pierced the silence in the aftermath of the collapse. Arlo bounded up to Parker and licked her face. He smelled like the sweatiest dog in the world. She buried her head in his filthy fur and wept.

He pulled back and barked again, nipping her sleeve and tugging it until she stood up.

"OK, OK," she said, her voice a raspy croak. She coughed up dust. "You want me to follow you? You want to bring me to Ellie and Dad?"

Arlo let out a long whine. Parker went.

When they left the bounds of Haven, she tucked Walter's teapot in a shady area and removed the lid. "You'll be safe here until we come back," she whispered.

Then Arlo ran, and Parker followed.

Ellie was holding the train upright with a net of vines. They shot from the landscape, twining around her fingers and arms before slipping off and projecting away from her at her will. They unfurled in the air and sprouted offshoots that wove together like thick ropes until they wrapped around the train and tethered it to the cliffside.

But Ellie had been at it for a long time. Maybe twenty minutes. Maybe more. She had to hold her arms aloft to direct the position of the net, and her arms were growing weak. It felt as though she'd been holding them at shoulder-height for an hour or more. She wasn't sure she could continue. At the thought, the vine netting loosened, and the train pitched forward, screams of its passengers echoing around her.

Dad was in there.

Ellie pushed through the pain.

Then there was a frantic bark behind her, and the sound of her sister's footsteps.

Together, they could save everyone. Together, the plan could work.

Parker stopped short when she saw what Ellie had done. Long, thick vines shot from the earth and writhed in the air as her sister directed their tendrils toward the train as if she were a puppeteer and they were joined to her hands by invisible strings. At Ellie's bidding the vines forming a thick net that secured itself to the side of the mountain, acting as a sort of sling.

"I didn't know you could do that," Parker gasped, awed.

"I didn't either, until now," Ellie told her. "But I can't do it for much longer. Parker, I need you."

Parker moved next to Ellie. She took stock of the situation. The train had fallen from the tracks on the buckling bridge, where an enormous chunk of earth and rock had given way beneath it. Parker focused on the rock. She focused on making it whole again.

Little by little, the rock built itself back.

Out of the corner of her eye, Parker saw Ellie's arms shaking involuntarily. She knew she had to work faster if they were to save the people on the train. *Dad*.

Ellie heard her thought. Parker knew she did because she lifted her arms higher, made them stronger.

Then Parker saw something—*someone*—else in her periphery.

Boudin had approached. She gave Parker a small nod, then turned her focus toward the train.

Two more figures approached from Parker's left: Casey and Cassie Phillips.

Then Felix joined them, until they formed a formidable line of six.

Parker watched as the iron of the bridge bent and straightened.

It wasn't coming from her.

From afar, Parker thought they probably looked like six regular people watching a disaster unfold. Their intense focus could be mistaken for horror or awe.

But beneath their faces, Parker knew something much more extraordinary was happening.

She began to work more quickly, piecing the rock back into the hillside like a larger-than-life puzzle. Holding it there until the rock fused.

When it did, Ellie pulled the net with all her might. Parker heard her sister straining with the effort.

You can do this, Ellie, Parker thought at her, as Ellie dragged the train back onto the tracks.

When it settled, there was a silence.

Then a chorus of cheers rang out. A crowd of onlookers had formed—Parker had been too focused to notice. She turned to thank Boudin and the Phillips twins and Felix, who surely had helped—hadn't they? But they had disappeared into the crowd; she couldn't see any of them.

She turned to Ellie, who stared back at her, wide-eyed. They had really done it.

"You were amazing," Parker whispered. Passengers came pouring from the train. They watched them maneuver the track toward the station, where Parker and Ellie stood.

"I couldn't have done it without you," Ellie told her honestly.

"I know," Parker said. "I couldn't either. I wouldn't want to."

"Parker," Ellie whispered. "You didn't even have your bracelet on. What does it mean?"

Parker was quiet for a long minute.

"I think it means we don't need the bracelets to be powerful. At least not when we're working together. Or with others. Did you see Boudin and the twins and Felix? Were they—?"

Their dad spotted them at the same time they spotted him. He ran across the rest of the rails, stopping only to kneel down and scoop them both into his arms.

"You're safe," he said. "Thank God."

Ellie and Parker wrapped their arms around him. Arlo yipped behind them.

"From now on, we do things as a family," he said. "OK?"

"Yes," Parker replied, and Ellie laughed, nodding into his shoulder.

I did a lot of jobs today, Arlo remarked to Ellie. *How about a treat?*

CHAPTER TWENTY-ONE

"I can't believe Dad hired people to spy on us," Parker remarked to Ellie as they got ready for bed that night. Arlo's ears pricked from his position on the woven rug in the girls' room, and Walter jumped in his bowl, which sat atop Ellie's desk, causing a splash of water to crest over the bowl's side and dampen Ellie's notepad below.

"Our people, though. People like us. I can't believe you thought the librarian might be evil," Ellie said. "She was so nice to us! Anyway he didn't *hire* Boudin and the Phillips twins—they wanted to help protect us. Does Felix have powers too, then? Does that mean he has a twin?"

"I'm not sure." Parker shrugged. "We'll have to figure out a way to get in touch with him."

"Okay, but we can't just *ask* him. If he doesn't have powers and just happened to be observing, he'll think we're looney tunes." Ellie paused, reflecting. "It's so cool that it's not just us in this. Like we have built-in teammates for saving the planet."

Parker laughed. "Teammates, huh? Suddenly you like being a part of a team so much?"

"Sure, if I get to be on a team with my twin sis."

"That was so lame and cheesy," Parker told her, "but I love you too. By the way, I like sharing a room with you again." She pulled on her striped PJs, flopped onto Ellie's bed, then toyed with the brass compass she'd taken from Haven. "Can you believe the Phillips twins have powers too?" She flicked the compass open absently. "How cool is that?"

Parker stared at the compass. "Wow." She'd never really looked at it before since Ellie had been the one to hang onto it. Now she was astonished at the intricacy of its design. It was covered in ornate etchings: animals, flowers, a miniature solar system. "This is really cool," she commented. "How come I didn't think it was cool before?"

"Eh," Ellie said, drawing her legs to her chest. "I don't think you were ready to forgive Mom for leaving."

"Yeah." Parker was quiet, studying the compass. "Where do you stand on that these days?"

"I don't know," Ellie answered honestly. "I mean, I'd like to believe she's alive, but . . ." she trailed off.

"We saw what Mabel can do," Parker finished. "And if she was jealous of Mom's and Sadie's powers or thought she could fix the planet better if they were out of her way, she probably went for it."

"Yeah."

"I wonder if we'll ever know the truth."

"They're gone, now. So maybe not." Ellie reached for the compass. "Let me take a look at that." She examined the object she'd held a million times. There was a word written along the side, so small and faint she'd only just noticed it at Haven. "What does *animulus* mean?" she asked. "Is that the plural for 'animal' in Latin?"

"I don't know." Parker shrugged. "But who *will* know is my friend the Internet. God, I missed this," she said, picking up her phone and typing the term into the search bar. It occurred to Parker that she hadn't bothered contacting Clara yet. She had been so busy settling in with Ellie that she'd forgotten. Well, Clara could wait another day.

"Hmm," Parker said. "Apparently it means 'heart' or 'soul.'"

"Ohh," Ellie smirked. "Maybe it'll point us in the direction of your lost soul."

"Ouch," Parker said. "Thanks a lot."

Ellie squinted at the face of the compass. "Um . . . Parker."

"Yeah?"

"The needle is moving."

"Stop, Ellie," Parker yawned. "I'm wiped out. Not in the mood."

"It *is*," Ellie said, her voice rising. "Seriously. Look! It hasn't moved *ever* in *years*. Parker. This is freaky."

Parker leaned over and looked at the compass. Sure enough, the needle was tugging east just slightly. "What the . . ."

Just then, the doorbell sounded.

Ellie went pale. Their dad's footsteps moved across the ground floor.

"Who is ringing the doorbell this late at night?" he grumbled.

"Come on," Parker whispered. She and Ellie crept out of their room silently and made their way to the top of the staircase. Their father opened the door, then stumbled backward.

From their vantage point, Parker and Ellie could not see the visitor's face. Only her flowered sundress, which was tapered at the waist; her leather buckled shoes; and her slender wrists, one of which was encircled with two silver bracelets.

"You must be Edward," a woman's warm voice said. "I'm sorry, I realize this must be startling for you. I'm Sadie."

Their father was silent. Parker and Ellie exchanged shocked looks.

Is she good or is she bad? Parker thought at Ellie, out of convenience.

Ellie was mystified. "I don't know," she whispered back.

"May I come in?" The woman—Sadie—took a step inside and bent low so she could see to the top of the stairs.

Her face was so like their mother's it was uncanny.

"And *you* must be the invincible Powers," she said, laughing up at them. "I've heard quite a lot about you, you know."

ACKNOWLEDGMENTS

We'd like to thank our partners, Chris and Trevor, who did what the best teammates do and encouraged us throughout this adventure. For the true "nature girl" in our family, Kristina, we are thankful every day for your enthusiasm, activism, knowledge, and pure love of our planet and its beauty. Thank you to Todd, Erica, and Dara for your belief in this story from the beginning and for helping us find its perfect home. Anne, thank you for your incredible support; you are magic. Thank you also to Mariko Tamaki for your thoughtful collaboration. Finally, a very special thanks to Aimee, Indy, Daisy, Maebe, Kitty, Farley, Drift, Jerry, and Marty, who taught and continue to teach us that every living thing can communicate if you listen closely enough, and whose companionship made us dream of a world where we can talk to animals.